D0069308

Star Friends

Secret Spell & Dark Tricks

BY LINDA CHAPMAN

ILLUSTRATED BY LUCY FLEMING

tiger tales

tiger tales

5 River Road, Suite 128, Wilton, CT 06897
Published in the United States 2023
Originally published in Great Britain 2018
by Little Tiger Press Limited
Text copyright © Linda Chapman
Secret Spell, 2018
Dark Tricks, 2018
Illustrations copyright © Lucy Fleming
Secret Spell, 2018
Dark Tricks, 2018
ISBN-13: 978-1-6643-4070-1
ISBN-10: 1-6643-4070-X
Printed in the USA
STP/4800/0501/0123
All rights reserved
2 4 6 8 10 9 7 5 3 1

www.tigertalesbooks.com

CONTENTS

Star Friends

Secret Spell

To Spike, who gives me so
many amazing ideas!—L.C.

To Katie—L.F.

Contents

1
IN THE STAR WORLD

A snowy owl, a badger, a stag, and a wolf
gathered by a waterfall of falling stars. Their fur
and feathers glittered with stardust, and their
eyes were a deep indigo blue. The owl hooted
softly. "My friends, let us see what is happening
with the young animals and their Star Friends
in the human world."

As he touched the surface of the pool with
the tip of his wing, an image slowly formed.
Four girls and four animals with indigo eyes
were settling down for the night. A girl with

dark-blond hair was hugging a fox, a girl with black curls was cuddling a red squirrel, a girl with long dark brown hair was petting a deer, and a girl with red hair was curled up beside a wildcat with a tabby coat.

"They all look happy," said the badger with a sigh of relief.

Hunter the owl nodded. "The young animals are doing well. They have been teaching their Star Friends how to use magic to keep the human world safe. The good deeds they have done so far have strengthened the magic current that flows between our world and the human world, and has made their magical abilities stronger."

The wolf stiffened. "The picture is changing!"

A new image formed, showing a person wearing a black hooded robe and holding a stone bowl filled with small objects. Shadows were swirling up from the ground.

The stag pawed the earth in alarm.
"Someone is working dark magic near the Star
Friends!"

The owl nodded gravely. "I'm afraid it appears
to be as we suspected. Two Shades have already
been defeated by the Star Animals and their
friends. But now more trouble is coming their
way."

The wolf growled. "I believe I know this

person we can see."

"You do, my friend," said the owl. "She has caused problems in the past. Her magic was once bound, but now she is able to use it again."

"What can we do to stop her?" said the stag.

"Nothing." The owl shook his head. "It is up to the new Star Animals and their friends to stop this threat. All we can do is watch."

"And hope the dark magic does not win," said the wolf grimly.

2
A TERRIBLE DREAM

Mia stood on a bridge. On one side, a dark mist rose from the ground. Mia's blood turned to ice as the mist took the shape of a tall, thin figure. It was a Shade—an evil spirit from the shadows who liked to hurt people.

As the Shade fixed its eyes on her, Mia looked around desperately. Where was Bracken, her Star Animal? And where were her friends and their Star Animals?

"Let me past!" the Shade hissed.

Mia stood her ground. "No!"

In a shimmer of starlight, a fox with indigo eyes appeared beside her.

"Bracken!" Mia whispered in relief.

Bracken leaped between Mia and the Shade. "Go back to the shadows!" he growled.

The Shade snickered. "Why should we listen to you? Only a Spirit Speaker can command us."

Mia's heart skipped a beat as more dark shapes started to form behind the first Shade.

They spoke with one eerie voice. "You may have defeated the Wish Shade, but the one using dark magic has conjured more of us. She wants us to make all your fears come true!"

Stepping forward, the first Shade swiped at Bracken, who yelped in pain as sharp nails scratched him.

"Bracken!" Mia screamed.

Mia felt something licking her nose.

"I'm here, Mia."

Hearing Bracken's voice, she blinked open
her eyes and looked into his anxious face. Then
she felt a hand on her shoulder and heard Sita
gently saying, "Mia, wake up."

Mia's heart gradually slowed. She was in her
bedroom with Bracken on her lap and Sita
kneeling beside her. Sita's Star Animal, a gentle
deer named Willow, was next to Sita, while
Lexi and Violet were still fast asleep on the
floor nearby with their Star Animals—a red
squirrel and a wildcat. The gray light of dawn
was just streaking across the sky.

"Were you having a bad dream?" Sita
whispered.

Mia nodded. "It was about a Shade." She shivered as she remembered. "A lot of Shades. Bracken got hurt. It was horrible."

Bracken licked her hand, and Mia wrapped her arms around him. She couldn't bear the thought of Bracken being injured. Ever since they had become Star Friends a few weeks ago, she had felt a deep bond with him—she loved him more than anything in the world.

It's like he's part of me, she realized.

The day she had met him in a clearing in the woods was etched into her mind. To Mia's amazement, he had talked to her, telling her he was from a different world and that if she wanted to be his Star Friend, he would teach her how to use magic to do good and make the world a better place. Most importantly of all, they had to stop anyone who was trying to use dark magic to hurt others. It had been even more amazing when her best friends had become Star Friends, too.

"You probably had a nightmare because of that horrible Wish Shade we fought last night," Sita said. "But Violet sent it back to the shadows, remember? It's gone. There's nothing to worry about."

As Mia felt her fear fade, she wondered if Sita was using her special magic abilities. The Star Animals had taught them all how to use the magic current that flowed between the human world and the Star World. The girls had found they each had different skills. Mia could see things that were happening elsewhere and look into the future; Sita could heal and soothe; Lexi was amazingly agile; and Violet could shadow-travel. Not only that, Violet was also a Spirit Speaker, which meant she could command Shades and send them back to the shadows.

Mia gave Sita a grateful look. "You're right. I'm sorry I woke you up."

"Mia, what did you see?" Bracken asked.

"Does it matter?" Sita said. "It was just a dream."

Bracken looked anxious. "I'm not sure. As Mia's magic sight abilities get stronger, there might be things in her dreams that come true."

Mia felt a flicker of alarm and tried to remember. "I was on a bridge, and the Shade said something about the one who had conjured the Wish Shade calling more Shades … and then more of them appeared. Then the Shade attacked."

"I hope it doesn't come true," said Sita. "It was scary enough facing just one Shade last night. I don't want to have to fight a bunch of them."

Just then, Violet sat up sleepily and pushed her red hair out of her face. "What's going on?"

Beside her, Sorrel the wildcat stretched and rolled onto her back. "I refuse to believe it's morning yet," she yawned. "Whatever it is, it can wait."

"No, it can't. This could be important. Wakey-wakey, pussycat," said Bracken, jumping over Sorrel's tummy and landing on the end of her fluffy tail. "We all need to talk."

The wildcat leaped to her feet and hissed. But Bracken ignored her and trotted over to wake Juniper the squirrel and Lexi, who were curled up together inside Lexi's sleeping bag. Juniper squeaked in protest and snuggled closer into Lexi's arms, so Bracken kept licking them both until they woke up.

Soon the girls were all sitting around in a circle, cuddling their animals.

"If Bracken's right and Mia's dream *is* true," said Violet, "then we have to try and find out who is conjuring these Shades."

"The Shade said it was a woman," Mia remembered. "And that she's the same person who conjured the Wish Shade."

"I wish we could use your magic to find out more, Mia," said Lexi.

Mia wished that, too, but she had already tried to see who had conjured the Wish Shade, and her magic had shown her nothing but darkness. Bracken had told her it seemed as though the person was using a spell to conceal herself.

"We should start by finding out who gave the little garden gnome with the Wish Shade trapped inside to Paige's family," said Violet. "We need to know if that person knew about the Wish Shade and that it was going to make wishes come true in a horrible way."

Mia nodded. "I asked Paige once, and she said

that the gnome was from a friend of her mom's. We need to find out her name." She jumped to her feet. "Let's go to Paige's house now."

Violet leaped up, too. "Yes, let's!"

"Wait!" said Lexi. "Everyone will still be in bed."

"Oh, yeah," said Violet, looking disappointed.

Mia sighed. Now that they had a plan, she wanted to act on it right away.

"While we're waiting, you could all try doing some magic," Bracken said. "Mia's magic seems to have gotten stronger from defeating the Shade yesterday, so maybe everyone else's will have, too."

Juniper jumped onto Mia's desk, his tail curling behind him. "You might all be able to do new things!"

"Oh, I hope so! I can already do so many cool things with my magic. Imagine if I could do even more," said Violet.

Mia saw Lexi roll her eyes. Violet sometimes

said things that made her sound boastful, and it really irritated Lexi. It used to annoy Mia, too, but now Mia was beginning to think that Violet didn't mean to show off; she just didn't always think about how what she said would sound to other people.

"We could go to the clearing," said Willow.

Bracken yapped in agreement, Juniper chattered happily, and Sorrel nodded her head. The animals all loved the clearing in the woods. It was where they had first appeared when they had traveled from the Star World, and it was an especially magical place.

Juniper leaped onto Lexi's shoulder. "When we're at the clearing, we might also find out which of you is the super-strong one the Wish Shade spoke about."

Mia felt a jolt run through her. Just before the Wish Shade had been sent back to the shadows, it had told them that one of them would turn out to be incredibly powerful—

so powerful that the person using dark magic would be scared of them.

"I'd forgotten about that," said Sita.

"Me, too," said Lexi.

"It's obviously going to be Violet," declared Sorrel. "She can shadow-travel and command Shades already."

Violet looked happy.

"It might not be Violet," protested Lexi. "It could be Mia or Sita."

"Oh, I don't want it to be me," said Sita hurriedly. "I'm happy just healing people."

"It could be you, Lexi," Mia put in. "Your agility is incredible. I wish I could run and jump and climb like you."

Bracken put his paws up on Mia's leg. "I bet you're the special one, Mia," he whispered.

Mia hugged him. She really hoped so!

Sorrel trotted to the door, her tail ramrod straight. "Why are you all standing around talking?" she said. "Let's go!"

3
A Little Magic Practice

The girls pulled on their clothes. As they left Mia's bedroom, the animals vanished—it was important for them to stay secret from other humans.

Violet fell into step beside Mia as they went downstairs. "This is really exciting, isn't it?" she said in a low voice. "We might all have new powers. And it sounds like there will be more Shades for us to fight."

Mia nodded in agreement. Although Shades were scary, she felt a thrill at the thought of using her magic to stop them. "Last night was exciting, wasn't it?" she said to Violet.

Violet grinned. "Chasing a possessed gnome, rescuing friends from a burning shed, and using magic to fight an evil Shade…. I mean, who'd want to do anything else on a Saturday evening!"

Glancing at Violet's happy face, Mia remembered something Sita had said—that she thought Violet had been lonely and was really enjoying hanging around with them now that they were all Star Friends. Mia was beginning to feel Sita was right.

When they went into the kitchen, they found Mia's little brother, Alex, sitting in his high chair.

"Morning, girls!" Mr. Greene said cheerfully. "Nice to see you up so bright and early."

"We were going to go out for a bike ride," Mia said.

"Okay, but have some breakfast first."

"Bek-fast!" called Alex, offering his sister a piece of his toast.

Mia grinned. "Thanks, Alex, but I'll get my own."

Alex threw the toast on the floor. "All gone." He giggled.

"Come on, young man," Mr. Greene said, undoing the harness and scooping Alex up out of the high chair. "We're going to rake some leaves in the yard together."

Alex shook his head firmly. "No leaves. No beetles."

"Don't be silly. Beetles won't hurt you," his dad said.

"No beetles! No!" Alex's voice rose, and he struggled in his dad's arms.

"He's scared of beetles," Mia explained to the others as they got out the cereal boxes. "He was helping Dad the other day, and they found a nest of beetles under a pile of leaves."

"All right, Alex, all right," Mr. Greene said soothingly. "You can play in the sandbox then."

Alex continued to struggle. "No yard! No!"

Sita went over and took his hands in hers. "Oh, Alex, don't worry. The beetles will leave you alone. You can have a nice time playing in the sandbox." Alex stopped wriggling and stared at her as she spoke. "You can play with your shovel, can't you?" Sita went on, her gentle brown eyes fixed on his.

"Play," Alex repeated, gazing at her. Then he looked up at his dad. "Me play outside."

Mr. Greene blinked. "Okay, great." He turned to Sita. "You really have a knack with little ones, Sita."

Sita smiled. "I get a lot of practice with my little brother."

Mr. Greene nodded. "Well, thanks," he said, and he carried Alex outside.

"Were you using your magic then?" Mia whispered to Sita.

She nodded and grinned. "Of course. Willow told me we should use it as often as we can to help people. Every bit of good we do strengthens the magic current."

"And our own magical abilities," added Violet.

They had just started to eat breakfast when Mr. Greene came back in.

"Mia, you haven't seen the key for the shed, have you?"

Mia shook her head. "I'm sorry, no."

Mr. Greene frowned then went out again, muttering, "I don't know where it could be."

Mia thought for a second and then, remembering what Sita had said about using their magic to help people as much as they could, she picked up a spoon. Could she find the key? She turned over the spoon and looked into the shiny surface, opening her mind to the current of magic. She felt it flow into her, making her tingle all over.

"Show me the key to the shed," she whispered.

An image formed in the back of the spoon. It showed a key inside an old pottery vase. Mia recognized it as one of the flowerpots that sat just under the shelf where the key was usually kept. The key must have fallen into the vase!

She put down the spoon and hurried to the
back door.

"Dad!" Her dad was looking under the jam
jars and paint cans. "Have you looked in the
flowerpots? It might have fallen off the shelf."

"I did take a quick look," Mr. Greene said.

Mia's eyes fell on the vase, and she picked
it up and turned it upside down. A metal key
dropped out. "It's here! Look!"

"Oh, great job!" her dad said. "That was a
lucky guess."

"Yep," Mia said, hiding her smile. Being able
to do magic was awesome!

As soon as they had put away their bowls,
the girls set off on their bikes. It was a crisp
November morning, and the sun was just
starting to rise. The chilly breeze made their
cheeks glow, and Mia was glad she had put on
her scarf and gloves. The streets of Westport

had an early Sunday morning quietness about them. A few people were out walking dogs or running, but most of the houses still had their curtains drawn. The girls passed the playing fields where a huge bonfire was prepared.

"Are you all going to the fireworks tonight?" Mia asked as they rode past.

Her friends nodded.

"How about we meet there at six?" Sita suggested.

"I can't be there until six fifteen," said Lexi. "Can we meet then? I'll be with my math tutor until six."

Violet frowned. "Math tutor? Why do you have a math tutor? You're almost as good at math as me."

Mia groaned inwardly. Couldn't Violet tell that saying things like that would really irritate Lexi?

"Because I'm taking an entrance exam for high school in January, and my mom wants me to try and get a scholarship," Lexi retorted. "And actually I'm *just* as good at math as you!"

"Oh, look, there's Aunt Carol's house," Mia said hurriedly before Violet could reply. "Maybe we should stop by later and tell her what happened last night."

Aunt Carol was an elderly lady who could do magic—not with a Star Animal, but by using crystals. She had been one of Mia's grandmother's best friends, but Grandma Anne had died just a few months ago. Aunt Carol had told Mia that she knew all about Star Animals because she had seen Grandma Anne's Star Animal—a wolf—when they were children. Aunt Carol had said that she and Grandma Anne used to do magic together, and now she wanted to help Mia and her friends. Bracken and the other Star Animals weren't too sure about having the help of someone who wasn't a Star Friend, but Mia really liked being able to talk to Aunt Carol about magic and ask for her advice.

"Should we see if she's home now?" Violet asked.

"It's still pretty early," said Mia. "I'll see her later."

The girls rode across the main road and headed onto the track that led down through the wooded valley to the beach. Seagulls swooped overhead, and they could hear the distant sound of the ocean. The path to the clearing was halfway down the track, opposite Grandma Anne's house.

The girls left their bikes in the front yard.
The house was empty now—Mia's parents had
gradually been clearing out all her grandma's
things. Brambles caught at their legs as they
pushed their way along the overgrown
path, and the air smelled of fallen leaves and
dampness.

Emerging into the clearing, they called their
animals' names. The four Star Animals appeared
instantly. Bracken jumped around Mia, yapping
excitedly. Juniper scampered up a tree. Willow
cantered here and there, making playful little
leaps, and Sorrel rubbed against Violet's legs,
purring loudly.

Mia kneeled down and Bracken jumped
onto her lap, licking her cheeks and snuffling at
her ears. She hugged his warm body. "It's magic
time," she told him.

"I wonder if you'll be able to do anything
new," he said.

Mia grinned and pulled a small mirror out

of her pocket. "Only one way to find out.
I'm going to try looking into the past." It was
something she had tried to do before but had
never managed.

Violet overheard. "Remember to relax!" she
called.

"I will, thanks," Mia said gratefully. When
she'd been struggling with her magic the week
before, Violet had given Mia some tips that had
really worked.

Mia remembered Violet's advice as she looked
into the mirror. Breathe in for five seconds, hold
her breath for five seconds, breathe out. Do
that again and again. Count backward from ten.
She felt a sense of calm settle over her. Bracken
snuggled against her legs and Mia stared at the
mirror, letting everything else fade away....

The surface of the mirror shimmered. What
did she want to see?

"Show me Grandma Anne," she breathed.
"Show me her with her Star Animal."

To her excitement, an image appeared in the mirror's surface. It was a young teenager dressed in old-fashioned clothes—brown pants tucked into socks and sturdy shoes, a brown V-neck sweater, and blond hair held back by a scarf. It was Grandma Anne! Mia recognized her grandmother from old photos she had seen. Grandma Anne was in the woods, and a slim silver wolf with indigo eyes was at her side. One of her hands was resting on the wolf's back, and in the other she held a small mirror. Mia caught her breath. It was the same mirror she was holding now—Grandma Anne had given it to her a year ago.

Her fingers tightened as she wondered if her

grandmother had suspected that she was also going to be a Star Friend. She'd talked to her so often about magic. Warmth flooded through her as she imagined how happy her grandma would be if she knew that Mia *was* a Star Friend now.

She let the image fade.

"Did you see your grandmother?" Bracken asked eagerly.

"Yes," she said. "She was with her Star Animal."

Bracken jumped around her. "This is great, Mia. Your magic really *has* got stronger!"

Mia looked around, wondering what the others were doing. Sita was talking to Willow, Lexi seemed to have vanished, and Violet was standing in front of…. Mia frowned. A table? What was a table doing in the clearing? It had a faint glowing outline.

"Violet!" she called.

Violet glanced over, but before Mia could say anything, she felt a hand tug her hair. She jumped. Lexi was standing behind her.

Mia blinked. "How did you get there?"

"I can run so fast I'm invisible," Lexi said with a grin.

Mia gaped. "That's awesome!"

"I would hardly describe it as *awesome*," Sorrel commented with a dismissive flick of her tail. "In my opinion, the ability to run fast has only limited uses."

"Oh, really," said Lexi. She leaped forward and disappeared. Two seconds later, Lexi was standing beside her again, and Violet was patting the side of her head in confusion. Lexi held out her hand to Mia. In her palm was Violet's hair clip. "I think being able to run fast has a lot of uses," Lexi said.

The table vanished. Sorrel hissed at Lexi. "You made Violet lose her concentration."

"What was she trying to do?" Mia asked. "Why was there a table there?"

"She was casting a glamour," said Bracken,

bounding over to where Violet was standing.

"Correct!" said Sorrel smugly. "Now that is *definitely* an awesome ability."

"What's a glamour?" Mia asked.

Sorrel sighed. "A glamour is when magic is used to create an illusion. Something appears, but really there's nothing there."

"A glamour can also disguise something," added Juniper.

Violet's eyes shone. "I hadn't been able to do it when I'd tried before, but now I can! Look!" She concentrated again, and a chair appeared.

"That looks so real," breathed Sita. "That's an amazing power, Violet."

Violet looked delighted.

"It is, although the glowing light makes it just a little bit obvious that it's an illusion," Mia pointed out.

"What glowing light?" said Sita, looking surprised.

Bracken nudged Mia's hand with his nose. "Mia, I think you can see the light because your magic abilities have to do with sight. To everyone else, it looks like a normal chair."

"Oh," said Mia.

Lexi linked arms with her. "I think it's just as cool to be able to see through illusions as to make them," she said with a pointed look at Violet.

"It will be a very useful ability," Bracken agreed. "The key to shattering an illusion is to refuse to believe it's real."

Mia looked at the chair. "You're not real,"

she said. The chair vanished. "Whoops, I'm sorry, Violet!"

"It's okay. I can make it come back again," said Violet. The chair reappeared.

"I don't believe in you," Mia said. It vanished again.

Violet giggled. For a few moments, they kept making the chair appear and disappear, then Violet stopped. "I want to try something else with my magic." She went and stood near a patch of shadows and beckoned for Mia to join her. "Come here, Mia. I need your help with this."

Mia went over curiously. What was Violet planning?

"Want to try and shadow-travel together?" Violet asked.

"You can take me with you?" Mia said in surprise. Mia had seen Violet transport herself from one place to another using shadows, but it hadn't occurred to her that Violet's magic could extend to other people.

"I'm not sure … but I'd like to try!" Violet's green eyes shone. "My magic feels much stronger today." She took Mia's hand. "Just relax." She stepped into the shadows. Mia stepped with her, and the world suddenly disappeared. The next second, she was staggering slightly as everything came back into view. She blinked. They were on the other side of the clearing!

"Oh, Violet, you exceptional girl!" exclaimed Sorrel in delight.

Violet grinned. "Did you see?" she called to Sita and Lexi.

"Yes," said Lexi shortly.

"That's great, Violet," said Sita enthusiastically. She frowned slightly. "Everyone seems to have gotten new powers except me."

"Healing is a wonderful power on its own," Willow told her. "I'm sure your magic will be stronger, and you'll be able to heal bigger wounds."

"Willow's right," Violet
said, going over to Sita.
"And you're really
good at calming people
down and making
them relax, too."

Sita smiled at her.
"Thanks. I wouldn't
want to be the one with
the mega-power anyway."

"I wonder which of us it
will be," said Violet thoughtfully.

"Well," Sorrel began,
"as I've already said, I think—" She was
interrupted by a rustle in the trees.

"Someone's coming!" said Bracken.

The animals all vanished, and the girls
watched warily. Who was coming into the
clearing?

4
THE STRANGER

An elderly woman hurried through the trees.
Her gray hair was cut very short, and she was
wearing a scruffy beige raincoat and green
walking shoes. She had a wicker basket covered
with an old towel on one arm.

She froze as she saw the girls. "What are you
doing here?"

The girls looked at each other, taken aback
by her sharp tone.

"Um … we just came here for a walk," said
Mia.

"Leaving litter, no doubt!" snapped the woman. She spotted an empty soda can on the ground and scooped it up. "See! I knew it!"

"That's not ours," said Mia. She'd noticed it earlier and had planned to recycle it when she got back home.

"Likely story!" snorted the woman. "You kids should go away! Stay out of these woods."

"Okay … um … we'll go then," said Mia, glancing at the others.

They backed away and hurried down the footpath.

"What a weird woman!" hissed Lexi as soon as they were out of earshot.

"I didn't like her," said Sita with a shiver.

"I've never seen her before. Maybe she's just

visiting Westport," said Mia.

Westport was a large town, but she knew most of the older people who lived there by sight.

"I think she just moved here," said Violet. "I've seen her coming out of the house next door to your Aunt Carol's a few times. The one that was for sale in the summer."

Mia's heart sank. "Well, if she has moved in, I hope we don't see much of her."

Just then Mia's phone buzzed. It was a text from her mom.

> Dad says ur all out for a bike ride. If u want a hot choc then come to the Copper Kettle at 10:15. We'll be there with Alex and Cleo. Mom xxx

It was just past 10:15 a.m. "Mom and Dad are at the Copper Kettle. If we meet them there, they'll buy us a hot chocolate. Should we go?"

The Copper Kettle was a cozy bakery on the main road. The friends left their bikes in the bike rack and headed inside. The bell jingled, and they were hit with the smell of freshly bakes cakes and warm coffee. Mia breathed in deeply. "Mmm."

Her mom and dad were sitting with Alex and Cleo, Mia's fifteen-year-old sister, at a window table. Alex was coloring, and Cleo was flipping through a celebrity magazine while Mr. and Mrs. Greene were drinking their coffees.

"Mai-Mai!" cried Alex.

Cleo glanced up briefly from her magazine before continuing to read.

"Pull up some chairs, girls," said Mr. Greene.

Mia and her friends squeezed in around the table. Mary, the Copper Kettle's cheerful owner, bustled over to meet them. She was short and plump with curly brown hair and a beaming smile.

"What can I get you, girls?"

"Four hot chocolates I think, please, Mary," said Mrs. Greene, looking at the girls, who all nodded.

"What about cake?" Mr. Greene said.

Mia and Violet asked for a slice of chocolate fudge cake each, Lexi chose a white chocolate brownie, and Sita asked for lemon drizzle cake. Soon they were sipping mugs of hot chocolate topped with whipped cream and tiny pink and white marshmallows and nibbling their cake.

"I told your mom we'd be here," Mrs. Greene said to Lexi. "She's going to come by and pick up you and Sita. I've got your sleeping bags and things in the car."

Alex had finished coloring and started trying to grab handfuls of the flyers that Mary had displayed on the windowsill.

"Put them down, Alex," said Mr. Greene. "Take this instead." He handed Alex a toy train, which he took happily, throwing the flyers on the floor.

Mia picked up the flyers. As she did, she noticed one that she hadn't seen before. "Look, this is for a new wildlife sanctuary," she said, showing it to her mom.

"We could go one weekend," Mrs. Greene suggested.

Mary overheard them. "You really should visit the sanctuary," she said. "My sister Jenny moved into town a month or so ago, and now she works there. She said they have squirrels, foxes, and badgers. They take in animals that have been injured and nurse them back to health."

"We'll definitely go," said Mia to the others, who nodded.

"I'd like to run a wildlife sanctuary when I'm older," said Sita.

"Me, too," said Mia.

"I want to work with endangered animals all over the world," said Violet.

"And I want to be a vet," said Lexi.

They talked about all the things they would do when they were older until Lexi's mom arrived.

"See you at the bonfire tonight," Mia said as Lexi and Sita put their bikes into the trunk of her car.

"Six fifteen," Lexi reminded everyone.

Mia turned to her mom and dad. "I might stop by and see Aunt Carol on the way home. Is that okay?"

"That's nice of you," her mom said. "Tell Aunt Carol I'll pop over to visit her soon."

Mia was relieved that her mom didn't want to come along—she had been hoping she would have the chance to talk to Aunt Carol alone. She and Violet got their bikes and rode down the street, then Violet went on to her house and Mia turned onto Aunt Carol's street.

Getting off her bike, Mia leaned it against the wall outside Aunt Carol's house.

A delivery man was knocking at the door of the house next to Aunt Carol's. He was carrying a large cardboard box. The front door opened, and a white dog ran out.

"Jack! Come here!" shouted a voice.

The dog only had one ear and half its tail was missing, but Mia didn't care. She loved all animals. She went to the top of the driveway to stop the dog from running out into the road and held out her hand, but the dog backed away, growling. Mia was surprised. Animals usually liked her.

"It's all right," she said to the dog. "I'm not scary."

The dog directed a volley of barks in her direction.

The delivery man gave the dog a nervous look. "He doesn't seem too friendly, does he?"

Just then Mia noticed a woman with short gray hair at the door. It was the lady from the woods!

"Stay away from my dog!" the lady snapped at Mia. "And get out of my yard!"

Mia backed away as the lady called the dog into the house and snatched the package from the delivery man, slamming the door behind her. To Mia's relief, Aunt Carol answered the front door on her first knock.

"Mia, how lovely to see you! I was just making some treats to take to the bonfire tonight. Are you all right?" she asked, looking at Mia's flustered face.

"Yes." Mia swallowed. She didn't like being shouted at.

"What's the matter?" asked Aunt Carol, ushering her in.

When Mia told her what had just happened, Aunt Carol patted her hand. "Oh, my dear, how horrible. I didn't like Mrs. Crooks the moment she moved in. She's done some very strange things. She had a large shed built in the yard and then put up a really high fence. She

hardly says a word if I see her, even though I've asked her a few times if she wants to come over for coffee. She's always going off into the woods at very bizarre times, too." She shook her head. "She's very odd."

Mia felt relieved that it wasn't only the Star Friends who thought the elderly lady was odd.

Aunt Carol led Mia into the living room. The surfaces were decorated with large, shining crystals and a stone bowl that had some glittering polished stones inside. "I'm afraid I haven't managed to find out anything more about this Shade that's causing all the trouble."

"Oh, you don't need to worry about that anymore," said Mia, remembering she had good news. "It's been sent back to the shadows."

They sat down, and Mia told Aunt Carol everything that had happened the night before.

"My goodness," said Aunt Carol, putting her hand to her chest. "You all did very well. How did you do it?"

"It was Violet," said Mia. "She's a Spirit Speaker."

"I see," said Aunt Carol thoughtfully. "Well, that's lucky for you. What about the others? You've never told me what they can do."

"Lexi has powers to do with agility, and Sita is good at healing." As Mia spoke, she felt a little uncomfortable. She knew Bracken didn't like her telling Aunt Carol things about the magic— he had been told that no one except for Star Friends should know anything.

Glancing around the room, she decided to change the subject. "Aunt Carol," she said. "How do you do magic with crystals?"

"Well, crystals and stones contain their own special energy. I hold them in my hands, and by concentrating hard, I can use it—a little like you drawing on the magic current. Different crystals and stones can do different things—some can heal, others see into the future, some will help calm an angry soul, and others bring good luck. I've spent my life figuring out how to use their power."

"Is there any other type of magic—except for Crystal Magic and Star Magic?" Mia asked curiously.

"There's dark magic, of course, when people draw power from the shadows," Aunt Carol shuddered. "I don't like even thinking about that. And some people can draw magic from plants— they gather herbs and plants and make potions." She smiled. "If you hadn't met a Star Animal, then maybe you would have discovered how to use magic in another way. In fact, I'm sure you could master Crystal Magic. Here." She went to the stone bowl and pulled out a glittering round, pink stone from the bottom. It seemed to glow with a faint golden light. "This is a Seeing Stone—let's see if I'm right." She held it out.

As Mia took the pretty crystal sphere, her fingers tingled, and she caught her breath.

Aunt Carol's eyebrows rose. "I can see you're feeling the magic. Seeing Stones can be used to look into the past. You told me you've been trying to do that with your own magic. Well, try with this. Just hold it, concentrate on it, and tell it what you want to see."

It was on the tip of Mia's tongue to tell Aunt
Carol that she had finally managed to see into
the past, but then there was a knock on the
door.

"Oh, that will be my friends from the
Christmas fair committee," said Aunt Carol.
"We're having a knitting party this morning to
make Christmas tree decorations to sell at the
fair." She nodded at the stone. "Slip that in your
pocket, dear. You can keep it."

Mia put the pink stone into her pocket.
"Thank you! I'd better go now."

"Are you and your friends going to the
bonfire tonight?" Aunt Carol asked.

"Yes," said Mia.

"I'll see you all there, then," Aunt Carol said.

Mia followed her into the hallway, and Aunt
Carol opened the door to three ladies, all with
baskets of yarn and knitting needles.

"Hello, dear," said Margaret, who was tall and
slim and knew Grandma Anne. "How are you?"

"Fine, thank you," Mia said.

"What are you up to today?" asked Josie, who ran the town preschool and had known Mia since she was a baby.

"Oh, a lot of different things," said Mia. "I'd better go. 'Bye, Aunt Carol!" she called hastily before the ladies invited her to stay and do some knitting!

Picking up her bike, she turned around and then froze. Two garden gnomes had appeared on either side of Mrs. Crooks's front door. Garden gnomes that looked just like the gnome that the horrible Wish Shade had been trapped in!

5
DETECTIVE MIA

Mia's heart thudded in her chest. The gnomes had rosy red cheeks, little pointed hats, and big smiles. They looked just like the gnome that the Wish Shade had been in, except one had a fishing rod and one had a rabbit in its arms. She had to investigate! Could these gnomes have Shades in them, too?

She checked that no one was around and, leaving her bike against the wall, she headed up the path. She crouched down beside them and poked them gingerly with a finger.

The front door flew open. "You again! What are you doing with my new gnomes?" said Mrs. Crooks.

"Um… I was just looking at them," Mia stammered, jumping to her feet. "They're really cute."

Mrs. Crooks's eyes narrowed. "Don't you go getting any idea about stealing them."

Mia was shocked. "I wouldn't."

"You stay away," Mrs. Crooks warned.

Mia backed up the driveway. Then, jumping on her bike, she rode away as quickly as she could. Her thoughts were spinning. What was Mrs. Crooks doing with those gnomes?

Icy fingers trailed down her spine. Could Mrs. Crooks be the person doing dark magic? Mia was so busy thinking about it that she almost didn't notice Paige bouncing on the trampoline in her front yard.

"Hi, Mia!" Paige called, waving and then turning a somersault.

Mia skidded to a halt, remembering that they had been planning on asking Paige where the Wish Shade gnome had come from. "Hi, Paige. Are you okay today?"

Paige looked puzzled. "Yes, why?"

Mia lowered her voice. "After what happened with the gnome last night?"

"The gnome? What do you mean?"

Mia realized that when the Shade had been sent back to the shadows, the magic must have made Paige forget everything about it. The same had happened to her sister, Cleo, when they had sent back the Mirror Shade. "Don't worry," she said quickly. "But um … just one thing. You know the garden gnome that used to be here?"

"Yeah." Paige looked around. "Mommy must have moved it."

"Do you know where it came from?"

Mia asked hopefully.

"One of Mommy's friends gave it to us," Paige said. "She brought it over and put it in the yard. It was a lady with gray hair.... I can't remember her name. I think it was a present to say thank you to Mommy for helping with something." She grinned. "Mommy said she'd rather have had some chocolates!"

Mia's heart beat faster. Mrs. Crooks had gray hair! "Are you sure you can't remember her name?"

Paige shook her head. "No. Why?"

"It was just that I thought I might get one like him for my dad," Mia fibbed. "If you remember the lady's name, will you let me know?"

"Yep," said Paige, starting to bounce on the trampoline again. "I will. I think Mommy said she was just a friend from town."

Mia said good-bye and continued home. Mrs. Crooks had gray hair, but Aunt Carol had said that Mrs. Crooks had turned down her invitation to join her for the knitting party. Had Mrs. Crooks given the Wish Gnome to Paige's family, or was it someone else? Maybe someone who hadn't known there was a Shade trapped inside it? Mia turned things over in her mind and rode faster. She had to get home so she could talk to Bracken. She was sure Mrs. Crooks was involved—but how?

✦ ✦ ✦

As soon as Mia reached her bedroom, she shut the door and whispered Bracken's name. He appeared in front of her, bouncing around. Mia sat on the bed, and he jumped up beside her.

"What's been happening?" he asked. He always seemed to know when she had things that she needed to talk about.

"I saw Paige," Mia said quickly. "She can't remember the name of the person who gave the Wish Gnome to her mom, but she said it was a lady from town. Also there's an elderly lady who has moved in next to Aunt Carol. She's odd and has a strange dog, and when I came out of Aunt Carol's house, I saw two gnomes on her doorstep—just like the Wish Gnome! Could she be the person who's doing dark magic?" Mia said.

"She might be planning to put Shades inside the gnomes," said Bracken anxiously.

"That Shade in my dream said more Shades had been called from the shadows. I'd better tell the others." Mia reached for her phone but then paused. It was too risky to send a text just in case one of their parents checked their phone. "I'll tell them tonight at the bonfire," she decided. "If only Paige could remember the name of the person who gave the gnome to her mom!"

"Maybe you could use your magic to find out," Bracken said thoughtfully. "I know it didn't work when you asked to see who trapped the Shade inside the gnome…. But how about asking it to show you who *gave* the gnome?"

"That's a great idea!" Mia said. She put her

hand in her pocket to pull out the mirror, and her fingers brushed against the round pink stone that Aunt Carol had given her. She decided not to tell Bracken about it—she had a feeling he wouldn't approve of Aunt Carol suggesting she try doing magic in other ways. Leaving the stone in her pocket, she took out the mirror.

"Show me the moment the Wish Gnome arrived at Paige's house," she whispered.

The surface swirled with light, and an image appeared in the glass. Mia peered at it eagerly. She caught sight of a figure in a long coat but then, to her disappointment, the image blurred.

"Show me who gave the Wish Gnome to Paige's family," she whispered again.

But the image stayed blurry. "It's not working today," she said to Bracken. "I can't see clearly."

He licked her cheek. "Try again later."

Mia tried again several times that day, but each time, the mirror failed to show her what she wanted to see. In the end, she had to give

up and get ready to go out
for the fireworks.

"Have fun," Bracken said,
licking her nose. "I'll see you
when you get home."

Mia hugged him, then he
vanished. As she took off her
jeans to change for the bonfire,
the Seeing Stone Aunt Carol had given her
fell out of her pocket. She picked it up. It was so
pretty. Would she be able to do magic with it?

She rubbed the stone and felt the magic in it
prickle her fingers. Maybe she could use it to see
who had given the gnome to Paige's family. What
had Aunt Carol told her she needed to do?

No. She stopped herself. It felt wrong to try
and do magic with the stone without telling
Bracken. Reluctantly, she put it down on her
desk. She would tell Bracken about it later, and
together they could decide what she should do.

6
BONFIRE NIGHT

The night was cold and frosty, and the air was
full of the smell of smoke as Mia walked up to
the baseball field with her family. She usually
liked the smell of smoke from a fire, but now it
made her think about the Wish Shade trying to
burn down the shed in Paige's yard when she,
Lexi, and Sita were all locked inside. Horrible
pictures flashed through her mind—the Wish
Shade they had fought, the gnomes outside
Mrs. Crooks's house, the dream she had about
more Shades coming....

She spotted Lexi, Sita, and Violet and told her mom she was going to meet them. "We need to talk," she hissed as she hurried over.

"About what?" Violet said.

Sita's eyes widened. "Did you see Paige?"

Mia nodded, but before she could say anything, she was interrupted.

"Hello, girls," Aunt Carol said. She took some boxes of sparklers out of her purse. "Mia said you'd be here, so I thought I'd bring you all a little present. There's a box each."

"Thanks, Aunt Carol," said Mia.

"I love sparklers," Violet said. "Thank you!"

"Look, the boxes have a free gift with them!" said Sita. Each box of sparklers had a little yellow stretchy man taped to it.

"Cool!" said Lexi.

Aunt Carol peered at them. "How strange. I don't remember seeing those when I bought them."

Lexi took the little man off her box and waggled its legs and arms. "Do you remember the craze at school when all the boys had these? They kept throwing them at the walls to stick and the teachers got really angry."

Just then, Mia's mom and dad walked over with Alex on Mr. Greene's shoulders. "Hi, girls. Do you want some sparklers?" asked Mia's mom.

Mia's heart sank. Now there was no way she would get a chance to talk to the others. "It's okay, thanks. Aunt Carol just gave us some," she said.

"That's really kind of you, Carol," said Mia's mom.

"It's no problem at all, dear. Now I'd better go and help with the teas and coffees. Enjoy the fireworks, everyone!"

With a cheerful wave, Aunt Carol disappeared into the crowd.

"Carol's getting a lot more involved with town life than she used to," Mrs. Greene said to Mr. Greene.

"She must be lonely without Grandma Anne," he said. "They used to spend so much time together, didn't they?"

"Well, I'm glad she's keeping busy," said Mia's mom.

Alex suddenly spotted the stretchy man in Lexi's hands. "Me! Me!" he said, reaching out.

"No. They belong to the girls, Alex," said Mia's mom.

"Me want!" Alex's voice rose.

"It's okay. He can have mine," said Mia,

taking the stretchy man off her box of sparklers and giving it to her brother.

Just then, there was a shrill sound and a crackle as multicolored stars exploded into the dark sky.

"The fireworks are starting!" said Mia's mom.

Violet pulled Mia slightly away from the adults. "You were going to tell us something," she whispered.

The fireworks exploded overhead with a bang and a fountain of silver and gold stars. Mia shook her head. It was much too noisy to talk now, and there were people everywhere.

"I'll tell you tomorrow," she hissed. "Let's meet at the playground before school starts."

Violet nodded, and another firework erupted in the sky.

Mia woke early the next morning. To her relief, she hadn't had another nightmare about the Shades.

She glanced at her clock. There was still half an hour before she needed to get up for school. Bracken was snoozing beside her, his body stretched out along the comforter, his snout resting on her arm. She rubbed his head, and he wriggled up the bed and nuzzled her cheek with his cold nose. She giggled. "That tickles!"

Bracken rolled onto his back so she could scratch his tummy. "What are we doing today?" he asked.

"I've got school." Mia sighed. She glanced at her desk and saw the round pink stone there, glowing faintly in the dim light. She went over and picked it up.

"What do you have there?" Bracken asked.

"It's a Seeing Stone." Mia felt awkward.

"Aunt Carol gave it to me yesterday. She said I can use it to look into the past."

"But you don't need a Seeing Stone," said Bracken. "You can look into the past using the Star Magic."

"I didn't get a chance to tell her that I'd managed to do that," said Mia. "Maybe I should just try with this stone…. It might be easier." She gave him a hopeful look.

"Don't," Bracken said uneasily. "It doesn't feel right to me. You're a Star Friend. You should use Star Magic."

"Okay," Mia said. She sat down at her desk and dropped the stone into her lap. "I'll try this mirror again." She stared at the mirror on her desk and asked it to show her who put the gnome in Paige's yard.

But just like the day before, the image flickered and was too blurry to see clearly.

"It's no good." Mia glanced at her bedside clock. "Why don't I just try with the stone?

Aunt Carol thought it would help."

"All right," Bracken said, but he didn't sound happy about it.

Mia picked the stone out of her lap and gazed at it. "Show me the day the gnome arrived at Paige's house," she whispered. Excitement flared inside her as an image started to form inside it. Bracken paced around her chair, but Mia hardly noticed; she was much too busy staring at the image. Aunt Carol was right— she could do other types of magic! It felt different, though— as if her energy was being pulled into the pink stone.

She saw a woman in a raincoat with the hood pulled up, standing in the driveway of Paige's house by the trampoline. The person's back was to Mia, but then she half-turned. Mia gasped as she saw the Wish Gnome in her hands. She still couldn't see the woman's face clearly, but after she placed the gnome on the ground and stood up, the hood of the coat fell back, revealing short, iron-gray hair and a familiar face.

"Mrs. Crooks!" exclaimed Mia. She lowered the stone in shock. "Bracken! It was Mrs. Crooks!"

7
WHO IS MRS. CROOKS?

"I knew I didn't like that lady when I saw
her in the woods," said Lexi as they huddled
together in a far corner of the playground later
that morning. Their breath was freezing in icy
clouds on the air.

Mia nodded. "Mrs. Crooks hasn't been
in town long, and the Shades only started
appearing recently, too!"

"And there are two gnomes on her
doorstep?" said Sita.

Mia nodded. "Yes, and she's the person who

gave the Wish Gnome to Paige's mom! I saw
her with my magic."

"She has to be the one doing dark magic,"
said Violet.

Sita looked worried. "What if she puts
Wish Shades into more gnomes and gives them
to more people? Imagine all those people making
wishes that are granted in a horrible way."

"We don't know for sure that Mrs. Crooks
is the person who is conjuring Shades," Lexi
pointed out. "We really need proof."

"I could try spying on her house through my
mirror," Mia said. "I might see something that
would prove she's using dark magic."

"Why don't you all ask if you can come to
my house after school?" said Violet. "If Mia
can't see anything, I could shadow-travel to Mrs.
Crooks's house."

"That's too dangerous!" Sita protested.

"I can't meet tonight," said Lexi. "I have
gymnastics."

"We shouldn't do anything without Lexi," said Sita quickly. "It's not fair."

Mia glanced at Lexi. She didn't want to leave her out, but if Violet was right about there being more Shades, they had to do something fast. "Do you want us to wait until tomorrow?" she asked Lexi.

"No," Lexi said reluctantly. "You should find out what's going on. Tomorrow I have piano, so I won't be able to meet up then, either. I'm not free after school until Wednesday. But promise you'll tell me everything!"

"Promise. I'll stop by your house tonight and fill you in," said Sita.

"Okay. Be careful!" Lexi told them.

Mia took a deep breath. "We will."

After school, the girls shut themselves in Violet's bedroom and called their animals. They sat on the floor, and Mia took out her

pocket mirror. She felt the magic tingle through her.

Show me inside Mrs. Crooks's house, she thought.

An image appeared of a kitchen. There was a wooden table and two chairs, a dresser with some neatly stacked wildlife magazines, and a lot of brightly colored plastic bowls on the counter. Mia felt a flicker of disappointment. She wasn't quite sure what she had been expecting.

"I can see the kitchen," Mia told the others. "It just looks normal, though…." She broke off as the image in the mirror showed a door open. Mrs. Crooks came in, with the one-eared white dog at her heels.

"Time to go and check on the shed," she heard Mrs. Crooks saying. "They'll be ready to go soon."

Mia's eyes widened. *They'll be ready to go soon.* What was Mrs. Crooks talking about?

Mrs. Crooks bent down and rubbed the dog's head. "One day, they'll all be set free. That's what we want, isn't it?" The little dog ran to the back door and whined. Mrs. Crooks smiled. "All right. Let's go and see my beauties." She opened the back door, and they went out.

Mia slowly lowered the mirror.

"Well?" Violet demanded.

Mia's mouth felt dry. "Mrs. Crooks was talking to her dog about something she keeps in the shed. She said 'They'll be ready to go soon,' and something about setting them free."

Sita looked worried. "Do you think she has some Shades in her shed?"

"Can you look inside it?" Violet asked quickly.

"I'll try." Mia picked up the mirror again. *Inside Mrs. Crooks's shed*, she thought.

An image appeared. There was no light in the shed, and blinds were drawn across the windows, but Mia could just about make out some boxes. No. Not boxes. They were metal and wire-mesh cages. "There are cages in the shed!" Mia said to the others.

Sorrel hissed. "We need to investigate this more!"

Bracken leaped to his feet. "I agree! We need to look inside this shed."

"We might be able to spy on it from Aunt Carol's yard," said Mia. "Or even climb over the fence and get inside."

"Or shadow-travel inside," put in Violet.

"But what if there *are* Shades in there?" said Sita. "They might attack us. They've got such sharp nails, and they move so fast and—"

"Sita!" Mia put a hand on her arm. "Calm down."

Willow nuzzled Sita. "Don't be scared. We have to find out what's going on. It's what Star Friends do."

Sita took a trembling breath. "I know. I just hate Shades."

Mia squeezed her arm. "Don't worry. We'll all be together. Nothing bad will happen."

I hope, she added in her head.

8
SOMETHING STRANGE

Aunt Carol answered the door. "Hello, girls," she said in surprise.

"Can we please come in, Aunt Carol?" Mia said. "We need to use your yard."

Aunt Carol raised her eyebrows but ushered them inside. "So what's this about?" she asked as she shut the door.

"We think Mrs. Crooks might be the person conjuring the Shades," said Mia.

"No!" Aunt Carol gasped.

Mia nodded and told Aunt Carol about

the image of Mrs. Crooks with the gnome in Paige's yard. She explained what she had heard Mrs. Crooks saying and told her about the cages in the shed.

"I never liked that woman," said Aunt Carol, shaking her head.

"We need to try and find out exactly what's in her shed," said Violet. "Can we use your yard, please?"

"Of course. You can call your Star Animals, too, if you want," said Aunt Carol. "After all, it's not like you have to keep them a secret from me!"

"Thank you!" Mia said. She would feel much happier if they could have Bracken, Sorrel, and Willow with them.

They hurried through the house and out the back door to the yard. They whispered the names of their animals, and Bracken, Sorrel, and Willow appeared.

Mia heard Aunt Carol's intake of breath and

saw the elderly lady looking at the animals with a strange expression.

Bracken shot Mia an uncertain look.

"Oh, don't you worry about me, dear," said Aunt Carol, backing into the house. "I'll stay out of your way." She disappeared into the house and then reappeared at the kitchen window.

"Mia!" Bracken said anxiously. "You know people shouldn't see us unless they're Star Friends."

"It's only Aunt Carol, and she's seen Grandma Anne's Star Animal. Don't worry," said Mia.

"I smell Shades," said Sorrel, scenting the air. Her tail fluffed up. "All around here."

Willow went to the fence that separated Aunt Carol's yard from Mrs. Crooks's. "I can smell it here."

"The fence is too high for us to see over," Mia said. "If only Lexi was here, she'd be able to climb the fence."

"Lexi isn't the only one who can climb," said Sorrel. She jumped up and dug her claws into the side of the fence. In a few seconds, she was balancing on the top. "I can see the shed," she told them. "It's just on the other side. I'll try and see through the windows." She jumped down into Mrs. Crooks's yard.

Violet stepped toward a nearby patch of shadows.

"No!" Sita said, grabbing her. "Don't shadow-

travel there, Violet. It could be dangerous. Let's
wait and see what Sorrel finds out."

Violet looked like she was about to argue.

"Please stay," Sita repeated.

To Mia's surprise, Violet nodded. "Okay."

A few moments later, Sorrel reappeared
at the top of the fence. "This yard
definitely smells of Shades," she
said, jumping down and wrinkling
her nose in distaste.

"What did you find out?"
Violet asked eagerly.

"Not a lot. I saw the cages
through a gap in the shed wall, but
I couldn't see into them. Oh, and there
are gnomes in the yard."

"Gnomes," Mia echoed.

"Yes. Just like that one the Wish Shade was
in. A bunch of them."

Mia shook her head. "This is weird."

"We need to get into that shed," said Violet.

"I'll shadow-travel into the yard and see if I can get inside."

Violet stepped toward the shadows, but as she did, Bracken's ears pricked up. "Wait! I hear the back door." He cocked his head to one side, listening. "Mrs. Crooks just came into the yard!"

Violet looked at Mia. "What do we do? I could use an illusion—disguise myself in some way and get into the yard. Or I could shadow-travel here tonight and look into the shed then."

"But you'd be on your own," Sita pointed out. "It's too risky." She took hold of Mia's and Violet's hands. "Look, I know you both want to do something right now, but remember how dangerous Shades are. And this time there might be a lot of them. Please don't do anything just yet. Let's talk to Lexi and Juniper first."

Mia wanted to argue, but maybe Sita was right. She found herself nodding and realized Violet was nodding, too.

"All right," Violet agreed.

"We'll wait," said Mia.

"Okay, good," said Sita, looking relieved. "I'll tell Lexi what we've found out. And then we can think of a plan."

Mia racked her brain, but by bedtime, she still hadn't thought of a way they could safely get into Mrs. Crooks's yard and see inside the shed. She tried spying on Mrs. Crooks, but all she saw was her making an omelette and watching a wildlife program on TV—nothing to suggest that Mrs. Crooks was doing dark magic.

As she snuggled in bed that night, she pulled Bracken close. "I hope I don't have any horrible dreams tonight."

He licked her cheek. "I'll wake you if you do."

She kissed his head and went to sleep with him curled up against her tummy.

She didn't have a nightmare, but her dreams

were full of strange images again—Sita staring at a patch of shadows in alarm, Lexi pacing anxiously around her bedroom, Violet sitting on her bed looking unhappy, a person in a hooded cloak, tiny figures scuttling through the shadows, and a night sky where the stars formed into words: *her power grows.*

When Mia woke up, she rubbed her eyes and yawned. She felt tired even though she had just had a whole night's sleep. She wondered what the images meant, especially the last one. Whose power was growing? Was it one of them or the person doing dark magic?

She gave Bracken a hug and then got up and went downstairs.

Her mom was in the kitchen with Alex on her lap.

"Morning," said Mia.

"Morning," said her mom, yawning.

"Are you all right?" Mia asked, thinking her mom looked just as tired as she felt.

"Alex kept having nightmares," said Mrs. Greene. "I think the fireworks upset him."

"Not fireworks. Beetle," said Alex solemnly. He cuddled closer to his mom. "Big beetle." He looked at Mia with wide eyes, and his lower lip trembled. "In my room!"

"It was just a bad dream, Alex," Mia said. "There are no beetles in your room."

Alex didn't look convinced. "Beetle," he said again.

"I know!" Mia hurried to the cupboard under the stairs where they kept all sorts of random things like gloves, umbrellas, and picnic blankets. She rummaged through one of the shelves and found what she was looking for. A plastic bug catcher! She'd liked to play with it when she was little, pressing the lever and clamping the plastic jaws around her toys. She took it back to Alex. "Here. If you see a beetle, you can pick it up with this and get rid of it." She picked a toy train off the floor to show him how it worked.

"Me do it!" Alex wriggled off his mom's lap and took the bug catcher from Mia, his nightmare forgotten.

"Thanks, Mia," her mom said with a smile.

Mia made herself some breakfast and then got ready for school. She desperately wanted to see the others. Maybe they had had some ideas. She sent them a text.

See u all at school before the bell! Mxx

A reply pinged back from Violet almost instantly.

Definitely! Can't wait to see u! xxxxxxx ☺☺☺

Mia blinked. Violet's texts were usually short, and she almost *never* used that many kisses and emojis. What was going on?

Her mom dropped her off early. The school playground was still almost empty. Violet was sitting on the wall at the edge of the playground. She came running over eagerly. "I thought you were never going to get here!"

Mia was surprised. "It's still early."

"I know, but I was worried." Violet's face took on an anxious expression that was very out of character. "You do still want to be friends with me, don't you?"

"Of course. Why?" Mia said in astonishment.

"Oh, nothing." Violet looked relieved. "It's just I had a dream last night that none of you wanted me to be a Star Friend. It felt so real." The anxious look crossed her face again. "It's not true, is it?"

"No," Mia reassured her. "Of course not. Everyone likes you. Although you might want to stop telling Lexi that you're better than she is at math," she added. "I think that annoys her

just a little bit."

Violet looked horrified. "Oh, no! I didn't mean to annoy her."

Mia was saved from replying by Sita arriving at the playground.

"Hi." Sita glanced over her shoulder as she reached them.

"Are you okay?" Mia said.

"Not really. I thought I saw something in the shadows when I was walking to school," whispered Sita. "It looked like a Shade!"

"A Shade!" echoed Mia and Violet.

"I thought I saw one last night, too," Sita told them. "It was in my room when I turned off my light. It was there for a minute, right by my closet, and then it disappeared."

Mia frowned. "What about Willow? Did she sense it?"

"I called her, and when she appeared, she said she could smell a Shade, but the scent was faint and it didn't seem to come from near the closet. The Shade had seemed so real and—"

She was interrupted by Violet suddenly waving madly. "Lexi, hi! Over here!" she called as Lexi came onto the playground. Lexi hurried over.

"Lexi! I never meant to upset you. I think you're great at math—really, really great!" Violet burst out.

Mia stared. It was like an over-friendly alien had invaded Violet's body! For a moment, she wondered if it could be a Shade…. But no, it wasn't making Violet horrible. It was making her super-nice.

Lexi looked surprised.

"You are so good at it," Violet carried on.

"No, I'm not," said Lexi gloomily. "I couldn't sleep last night. I kept thinking about that math challenge we did. I'm sure I've done badly on it. I think I failed my piano exam, too. What if I failed them both? I'm not looking forward to getting the results."

"You never fail anything," said Mia. "You'll be fine. Look, we need to think about Mrs. Crooks. Did Sita tell you everything last night?"

Lexi nodded.

"We need to get a good look inside that shed," said Mia. "Has anyone come up with any good ideas?"

"I bet you have," said Violet, smiling at her. "You're so great at thinking up ideas, Mia."

"Well, I haven't thought of anything yet," Mia

admitted. "Have you?"

Violet shook her head.

"Sita?" Mia asked.

"What?" Sita jumped as Mia said her name.

"Have you had any ideas?" Mia said.

"About what? About the Shade that's following me?"

"No," said Mia. "I really don't think there's a Shade following you. About Mrs. Crooks!"

"Oh … um … that," said Sita. "No, I haven't thought of anything."

"Me, neither," said Lexi. "The only things I can think about are my piano exam and the math challenge. I can't handle it if I've failed."

Mia felt like stamping her foot in frustration. What was up with her friends that morning? They were being really strange.

By the time school had ended, Mia had come up with a plan. If she and Sita distracted Mrs.

Crooks at the front door, Violet could shadow-travel into the yard and try and see into the shed. However, her plans were dashed when Violet's mom told them that Violet had a dentist appointment after school.

"I'll have to miss it, Mom," said Violet. "We've got stuff planned."

"Oh, no," her mom said. "You can't miss the dentist."

Violet turned to Mia and Sita. "Don't do anything without me."

"We won't. We'll wait until tomorrow," Mia said. Even if they had wanted to, they needed Violet's shadow-traveling to make the plan work.

"Lexi will be able to meet up with us tomorrow, too," said Sita.

"So you promise you won't go off and do anything without me?" said Violet.

"I said we wouldn't!" Mia spoke slightly sharply.

"Now you're annoyed with me!" wailed Violet.

"I'm not!"

"You are."

"Come on, Violet," her mom insisted.

Violet reluctantly left, shooting backward glances at her friends.

"I have no idea what's up with her today," Mia said to Sita.

"She is being odd," agreed Sita. "I'm glad we're not going to Mrs. Crooks's house, though. What if there are Shades in the shed?"

"Then we have to deal with them," said Mia firmly. "If Mrs. Crooks is doing dark magic, we have to stop her, Sita. You know we do."

Sita swallowed. "Y-yes. I guess."

Mia sighed. "I'll see you tomorrow."

"You're not going over to anyone's house today?" Mia's mom asked in surprise as Mia joined her. "That's unusual. How about we stop and see Aunt Carol then?"

"Okay," said Mia. "Where's Alex?" she asked.

"At home with Dad. He had such a bad night's sleep that he didn't go to his playgroup today. So how was school?"

"Okay," said Mia, thinking about how strangely her friends had been behaving. She couldn't wait to get home and talk to Bracken about it. Could it be because of some sort of dark magic?

When they reached the row of houses where Aunt Carol lived, Mia saw Mrs. Crooks's dog watching through her front window. He barked when he saw her, and Mrs. Crooks appeared. Seeing Mia, she scowled and closed the curtains. "Come on, Mia," her mom called as Aunt Carol answered her front door.

"How lovely to see you both. I have some friends here," said Aunt Carol. "We're planning the Christmas fair."

"Oh, we won't bother you, then," Mrs. Greene said.

"No, no, come in and have a cup of tea with us. Please."

Mia's heart sank. The ladies all greeted her and her mom warmly.

"I'll just put the kettle on. Mia, would you like a hot chocolate?" Aunt Carol said.

"Yes, please," said Mia.

"Why don't you come and give me a hand?" said Aunt Carol.

Leaving her mom to chat, Mia went into the kitchen with her. "So," Aunt Carol lowered her voice to a whisper and beckoned Mia closer. "Have you found out anything else about you-know-who?" She gestured toward Mrs. Crooks's house.

"No," Mia whispered back. "Not yet."

"I've been watching her. She went out late last night with a basket. I think she might be collecting herbs and plants to do magic with.

Shades can be conjured using potions. Did you know that?"

Mia's heart beat faster. "No."

"We need to keep an eye on her," said Aunt Carol. "She could have a secret place she goes to when she wants to work magic."

"In the woods, maybe?" Mia said.

"It's very likely," Aunt Carol agreed, nodding. "I'll try and watch her using my crystals. Have you tried doing magic with the Seeing Stone I gave you?"

"Yes, and it worked!" Mia said. "I saw into the past. That was how I saw Mrs. Crooks with the gnome at Paige's."

Aunt Carol smiled. "Great job. You're obviously very talented at magic."

Mia glowed. "Do you really think so?"

"Yes, I do," Aunt Carol said. She gave her a curious look. "Why do you ask?"

"Well, it's just that one of the Shades we

fought said that one of us would be really powerful—more powerful than the person doing dark magic."

Aunt Carol leaned closer. "Did the Shade say which of you it would be?"

"I don't know. He didn't—" Mia broke off as her mom came in.

Mrs. Greene laughed as they both jumped. "What are you two whispering about?"

Aunt Carol chuckled. "Oh, it's just a silly little secret we have," she said, tapping her nose and looking at Mia. "Isn't that right, Mia?"

Mia nodded.

Aunt Carol smiled brightly at Mrs. Greene. "Let's have some tea!"

9
DARK MAGIC AT WORK!

Mia was anxious to tell the others what Aunt
Carol had said about people being able to
conjure Shades using potions, but when she
got to school the next day, they were all still
acting oddly. She found Lexi sitting on a bench,
her head buried in her spelling book. "We've
got a test today. I'm sure I'm going to fail," she
muttered. "I can't talk now."

"Lexi, you're awesome at spelling. You
won't fail. I need to talk to you, though. This is
important!" Mia said.

"Not as important as my test." Lexi got up. "You don't get it!" She ran off.

Before Mia could go after her, Sita arrived. Her eyes were wide and scared.

"Mia! I'm sure there's a Shade following me!" she hissed as she raced up to her. "It was in our yard this morning and then behind some trees on the way to school. One minute it's there, the next it's gone."

"Let's go to the wall and talk there," said Mia.

"Okay, and there's something else I need to talk to you about, too," said Sita. "I'm sure it's not true, but Willow said I should mention it to you all."

As they walked over to the wall, Violet came running up.

"Where are you two going? Why weren't you waiting for me? You don't like me, do you? I knew it!" Her eyes filled with tears as she looked from Mia to Sita.

"Don't be silly!" Mia said in astonishment.

"Violet, I saw a Shade," said Sita.

"Where?" said Violet.

"In the trees, in the yard...."

Mia sighed. "Sita thinks he's following her, but...."

Violet glared. "So you've been talking about it without me? Leaving me out?"

"No!" Mia protested.

"I knew you didn't want to be friends with me!" Violet said, and fighting back a sob, she hurried away.

"Okay," Mia said in despair. "Why are you all behaving so strangely?"

"Look, in the shadows over there!" gasped Sita, pointing to a nearby hedge. Mia looked, but there was nothing there. She let magic flow into her and used her powers to see if there was anything she couldn't detect with her normal vision. Nothing.

"Sita, there really isn't a Shade there," she said. "I'm sure of it."

The bell rang, and Sita breathed a sigh of relief. "I'm going inside. It won't follow me there!"

Mia was beginning to think that somehow a Shade was affecting her friends. But what was it trying to do? Was there a type of Shade that just made people behave oddly? And if it was affecting her friends, why wasn't it affecting her?

Oh, Bracken, I wish I could talk to you right now! she thought.

After school, no one wanted to meet up. Lexi
wanted to go home in case the mail carrier
had delivered her exam results, Violet was still
refusing to talk to Mia and Sita, and Sita said
she wanted to stay with her mom.

As soon as Mia got home, she called
Bracken.

"What is it?" he asked her. "You look upset."

Mia hugged him and told him in a rush
what they had been doing.

"Why don't I go and talk to Willow, Sorrel,
and Juniper?" Bracken said. "If a Shade has
been anywhere near the others, Sorrel and
Willow will definitely have smelled it."

"Can you just go off and talk to them?" said
Mia. A thought struck her.

"I can call them using Star Magic, and
we can meet each other if we go to the
clearing," Bracken replied. "The clearing is
special because Star Magic is strong there. The
waterfall is a link between this world and the

Star World. I'll be back as soon as I can."

Mia kissed his head, and he disappeared.

Once he left, the minutes seem to drag by. She picked up her mirror. Maybe while she was waiting, she should use her magic.... But what would she ask to see?

Sita, she decided.

A picture of her friend appeared in the mirror. She was with Willow in her bedroom.

"I still haven't talked to the others about it, Willow," she was saying.

"You must," Willow said softly.

"But what do you think they'll say?" A noise made Sita jump. "The Shade! I just saw it again!"

"Sita, there's nothing there," said Willow.

Mia shook her head and tried Violet next.

Violet was sitting on her bed, her arms pulled tight around her knees. Sorrel was nudging her head against Violet's arm.

"No one likes me, Sorrel," Violet was saying.

"Mia and Sita keep going off and leaving me out."

We don't, Mia thought. *What's she talking about?*

"They don't want to be friends, and Lexi has never liked me," Violet went on. "I'm never going to have any real friends, am I?" She sounded so despairing. Her usual air of confidence had completely vanished.

"I'm your friend. I'll always be here for you," Sorrel said, her voice soft for once. "Please don't be upset, Violet. This isn't like you." She nuzzled Violet's cheek. Suddenly she stiffened, her head tilting to one side. "Violet, Bracken is calling me. I need to go. He wouldn't be calling me unless it was important."

Mia let the image fade and tried Lexi. She was pacing around her bedroom. "I'm going to fail, I'm going to fail," she was whispering. "Oh, what am I going to do?"

Juniper wasn't there. Mia wondered if he was

with Bracken and the others in the woods.

Mia put down the mirror. Her friends all seemed so unhappy. She ran her hands through her hair. She didn't know what to do about her friends, and she didn't know what to do about Mrs. Crooks. Were the two things connected?

Mia felt like she had pieces of a jigsaw puzzle laid out in front of her, but she just couldn't seem to put the picture together.

A few minutes later, there was a shimmer of light, and Bracken reappeared.

"I've spoken to the other animals, Mia."

"And?" Mia demanded.

"They all agree something strange is going on. Sorrel and Willow have both smelled the faint scent of dark magic in Violet and Sita's bedrooms, although they say the smell comes and goes. They're worried."

"What do we do, Bracken?" Mia said. "Should we try and find out what's going on with them, or should we try and find out more about Mrs. Crooks? If only the others weren't so distracted."

Bracken yipped and pricked his ears. "Mia! Maybe that's it! If Mrs. Crooks has somehow found out you're all Star Friends, she might be using magic to distract them."

Mia frowned. "But why just Lexi, Sita, and Violet? Surely she'd want to distract me, too."

Bracken's ears lowered. "Yes, you're right. That doesn't make sense," he admitted.

"Mia!" Cleo called from outside the room. "Mom says dinner is ready."

"Coming!" Mia got to her feet. "I'll be back as soon as I can," she promised Bracken.

Mia's mom had cooked lasagna for dinner, Mia's favorite, but she was so worried about what was going on that she didn't feel like

eating. Alex didn't seem to want his, either. He
pushed it around his plate and kept throwing
his fork on the floor.

"Come on, Alex, eat up," said Cleo, picking
up a spoonful of lasagna from his plate. "Here
comes the train. Choo-choo!"

"No!" Alex wailed, swinging his hand and
sending the spoon flying.

Mrs. Greene rubbed her forehead wearily.
"Don't worry, Cleo. He's just really tired."
Standing up, she lifted Alex out of his chair.
"Let's go and get you into your pajamas, Alex-
boy."

"I'll take him upstairs, Mom," offered Mia.
Her mom looked really tired.

"Thanks, sweetie." Mrs. Greene smiled.
"Once he has his pjs on, he can come down
and have some milk, and I'll read him a story."

Mia nodded and swung Alex onto her hip.
"Up we go," she said, heading for the door.

Alex clutched her as they reached the stairs.

"Beetle! No!"

"What do you mean, beetle?" she said.

He struggled. "In my room. Beetle!"

"There aren't beetles in your room, Alex. You just saw them in a nightmare."

"No." He shook his head. "Big beetle!"

They reached the top of the stairs. Mia put him down. "All right, if there's a big beetle, I'll get rid of it," she said. "Let me take a look." She pushed open the bedroom door. Alex's room looked just like it usually did. "See, no beetles."

Alex came slowly into the room. He stiffened and pointed at the closet.

"Beetle!" he whispered, his eyes growing wide as saucers.

"Don't be silly, there isn't a—" Mia broke off with a squeak as a large black beetle leg appeared out of one of the closet doors.

"Mai-Mai!" cried Alex, grabbing her around the knees.

Mia stared. What was going on? Suddenly, the closet doors flew open, revealing an enormous beetle with red eyes and sharp pincers. Rearing up on its back legs, it leaped out of the closet!

10
DISCOVERING THE SHADE

Mia hardly paused to think—she opened
herself to the magic current. When she was
using her magic, she could see where things
were going to move a second or two before
they did it. But the magic allowed her to
see something else, too. There was a glowing
outline around the beetle. It wasn't a real beetle.
It was just an illusion!

"I don't believe in you!" she said, pointing at
it. "You're not real."

The beetle paused.

"You are *not* real!" she repeated firmly.

The beetle vanished in a flash of light.

"Gone!" said Alex in surprise. "Beetle go poof!"

Mia breathed a sigh of relief. "Yes, beetle go poof!" she said. Crouching down, she pulled Alex to her and hugged him. "If it comes back, you just have to tell it you don't believe in it. You mustn't be scared—it's not real." She couldn't help wondering why on earth there was a beetle illusion in her little brother's room.

As she pulled Alex close, something fell out of his pants pocket. It was the stretchy man Mia

had given him at the fireworks display. Picking it up, she put it on his bookcase next to the bug catcher. "Come on, now, let's put your pajamas on."

She helped him get changed and took him back downstairs to their mom, then ran to her room and quickly told Bracken everything that had happened.

"I just don't understand," she said. "Why was there a beetle illusion in Alex's room?"

"It could be a Fear Shade," said Bracken. "They discover people's fears and use illusions to make it seem like those fears are coming to life. The more scared the person gets, the stronger the illusion grows."

"Do you think Fear Shades could be affecting Lexi, Sita, and Violet, too?" Mia said slowly. "Lexi's been really scared about her exam results, Sita's been terrified there's a Shade following her, and Violet…." She paused. "Well, Violet's been convinced we don't like her, but I'm not sure what that has to do with being scared."

"Unless she's scared about not having any friends," said Bracken.

Mia let out a breath. "Of course!" Violet might often act as if she didn't need anyone at all, but she'd been really happy since they'd become friends. Her fear *was* being without friends again. Suddenly, she remembered something. "Bracken! In my nightmare the other night, the Shades said, 'We will make your fears come true!' Well, people's fears *are* coming true—or at least it seems as if they are."

Bracken spun in a circle. "We need to find the objects the Shades are trapped in. What do all your friends have?"

"It has to be something Alex has, too." Mia shook her head. "I can't think of anything like that…." Then she gasped. "Oh, yes, I can! It's the little yellow stretchy men, Bracken! They were attached to the sparkler boxes that Aunt

Carol gave us on bonfire night. I gave my little
man to Alex, and the others all kept theirs. But
hang on—" she paused, frowning—"Aunt Carol
wouldn't give us something with dark magic
in it. Unless…." She started to nod as she made
sense of it. "Unless she didn't know. She said she
didn't remember the little men being attached
to the sparkler boxes when she bought them at
the store. Someone must have stuck them on
afterward! It could have been Mrs. Crooks, even.
After all, she lives next door!"

"We have to get a hold of those stretchy
men," said Bracken.

"There's one in Alex's bedroom," said Mia.
"Come on, no one's around."

They ran along the landing and into Alex's
room, and Mia shut the door. Her eyes fell on
the little yellow stretchy man sitting on the
bookcase where she had left it.

No. She frowned. She'd left it on the top
shelf, and now it was on the second shelf down.

Her skin prickled.

"Come here, you!" she whispered, reaching out.

The stretchy man jumped away from her. It scuttled along the shelf and then turned to face her. Its round face became pointed, its hands grew claw-like nails, and its face twisted into an evil smile.

With a growl, Bracken leaped at it, but it jumped down to the floor. Mia grabbed hold of it, but it bit her hard with its sharp teeth.

"Ow!" she gasped, dropping it.

It raced toward the door, but Bracken was there in a flash. He leaped in front of it and crouched down, blocking the way. "You're not getting out."

"Oh, I think I am," the stretchy man hissed. "I'll find someone else whose fears I can make

come true." He stretched his hands, and his nails grew even longer. "Move, fox, or you'll be sorry!"

"Not as sorry as you'll be for scaring my brother!" Mia grabbed the plastic bug catcher she'd given Alex and clamped the jaws shut over the stretchy man, trapping him inside. "Gotcha!" she said, holding him up.

"No!" the stretchy man screeched, hammering his little fists against the plastic container.

"Oh, yes, and now you and all the other Shades are going back to the shadows where you belong!" Mia picked up a metal tin that Alex kept cars in. She emptied it and dropped the stretchy man inside, releasing the jaws of the bug catcher and slamming down the lid.

Bracken spun in a circle. "Yay, Mia! You got him!"

Mia grinned. "One down, three to go!"

11
SITA'S SURPRISE

Mia persuaded her dad to drive her to Violet's house by telling him that they had some homework they needed to do together. She thought it would be best to go to Violet's first, then she and Violet could shadow-travel to Lexi and Sita's houses together. Violet's mom, Mrs. Cooper, answered the door.

"Hello," she said, looking a little puzzled. "Violet didn't mention you were coming over this evening."

"She didn't?" Mia said innocently. "We

arranged it at school."

"Well, come on in. She's in her room."

Mia hurried up the stairs and knocked on Violet's bedroom door.

"What is it?" Violet sounded upset.

"Violet, it's me—Mia."

"Mia?" The door opened. Violet's cheeks were tear-stained. "What are you doing here?"

Mia shut the door behind her. "Bracken!" she whispered. He appeared in a shimmer. "Call Sorrel," Mia urged Violet.

Violet looked confused but did what Mia said. "Sorrel!"

"What's happening?" said the wildcat as soon as she appeared. Her back arched, and she glared at Mia's bag. "Your bag smells like dark magic!"

"I'll tell you more about that in a moment," said Mia. "But first, Violet—"

"Why are you here?" interrupted Violet. "You don't like me. You, Sita, and Lexi don't want to be friends with me. I bet you all talk about me behind my back. None of you wants me to be a Star Friend." Her eyes brimmed with hurt. "You wish I'd never been chosen."

Mia wondered what to do. She'd been able to make the beetle vanish simply by saying she didn't believe in it, but Violet's fears were all in her head.

"Sorrel is the only friend I've got," said Violet miserably.

"That's not true!" Mia said. "Violet, I'm your friend. Please believe me."

Violet looked at her tearfully.

"It's true," said Bracken, licking her hand. "After you fought the last Shade, Mia told me how glad she was that you were a Star Friend and how happy she was that you were friends again."

"I think it's a Shade that's making you feel differently," said Mia.

"A Shade?" Violet echoed.

"Impossible," said Sorrel. "I would know if a Shade had been affecting Violet."

"You said you'd smelled the traces of a Shade here. Well, it's been moving around," said Bracken. "Probably so that you wouldn't catch it."

"Where is it?" said Sorrel, looking around. "What's it trapped in?"

"Violet, you know that little yellow stretchy man you got on bonfire night?" Mia said. "The Shade is inside it. There's one in my bag at the moment. We caught it at my house and put it in a tin. It made Alex think there was a giant beetle in his room."

"They're Fear Shades, I think," Bracken said. "Shades that make people believe their worst fears are coming true."

"Alex is scared of beetles, so he saw a giant beetle," said Mia. "Lexi's biggest fear is failing exams, and I think the Shade in her house is making her believe that's going to happen—"

"Sita's really scared of Shades, so her Shade has made her believe that there's one following her," Violet broke in. "And me … it's been making me think that no one likes me."

"You don't need to be scared of that!" Mia burst out. "We all like you. I mean, I know sometimes you and Lexi don't get along, but we all want you to be our friend. We're all glad you're a Star Friend—Lexi, too." She grabbed Violet's hands. "I promise I'm telling the truth."

As their eyes met, Violet swallowed. "I

believe you," she said slowly. Her expression gradually cleared. "I've been so silly!" she exclaimed, pulling away from Mia. "But the feelings I had seemed so real...."

Mia nodded. "The Shade made you believe them."

"Where is this Shade?" hissed Sorrel, her tail fluffing out.

There was a sinister chuckle, and a small, yellow stretchy man looked out from behind the mirror on Violet's desk.

"Looks like I've been discovered," he said. "And I was having such fun making Violet think everyone hated her. Tricked you!" He gave a squeaky laugh.

Sorrel sprang onto the desk. The stretchy man somersaulted off and lightly landed on the floor.

"Can't catch me!" he chortled.

He shot across the floor, heading for the slightly open window.

Bracken was after him in a flash, jaws snapping, but the stretchy man zoomed up the wall, using his sticky hands and feet. He reached for the window ledge and then recoiled with a high-pitched gasp as sharp spikes suddenly shot out of the windowsill.

"What?" he cried.

Losing his grip, he tumbled through the air, his limbs waving. As he landed on the floor, Sorrel sprang from the table and caught him in her jaws.

"Let me go!" squawked the stretchy man.

Mia pulled the tin out of her bag and opened the lid, and Sorrel spat the man inside. Mia banged the lid back on.

"What just happened?" the little man screeched.

"I think you'll find *I* just tricked *you*!" said

Violet. "You're not the only one who can cast illusions! I made you see what wasn't there!"

"No!" the little man shrieked, banging at the tin.

"Two down, two to go," said Mia, high-fiving Violet.

Sorrel gave a smug meow, and Bracken bounded over. "Now, that's what I call teamwork!" he said.

"Ugh!" Sita squealed as Violet and Mia suddenly appeared in the shadows by her closet. She and Willow leaped to the far side of her bedroom and stared at them with wide eyes.

"Violet? Mia? Is it really you?" Sita cried.

"Yes, we shadow-traveled here together," said Mia, going over to her. She looked at Bracken. "Bracken, guard the door. We'll have to vanish if anyone comes."

"I thought it was the Shade who's been
following me!" Sita said. "I—" She broke off
with a gasp and pointed to the closet.
"The Shade! Look! There it is!"

Hearing a low, sinister laugh,
they swung around. A tall figure
stepped out of the shadows. Its
limbs were angular, its fingers
tipped with spiky nails. "Sita,
oh, Sita," it hissed.

For a moment, Mia felt
her blood freeze. But then she
came to her senses. "You're not
real!" she said, marching over to
it. "I don't believe in you!" And
with that, the Shade vanished in a
cloud of smoke.

Sita gaped. "What … what's going
on?"

"The Shade was an illusion, Sita. There
hasn't really been a Shade following you,"

said Violet. "But there has been one affecting you."

"Where's the yellow stretchy man you got at the bonfire? The Shade is trapped inside that," said Mia.

"It's in my coat pocket downstairs," said Sita.

"Go and get it," urged Violet.

Sita hurried out of the room and returned a few moments later with her coat. She pulled the little stretchy man out of the pocket. "There's a Shade inside this?"

"Yes, one who's been making you imagine that a Shade is following you," said Mia.

As they spoke, the little man started to laugh. Violet snatched him from Sita before she could drop him. "The tin, Mia! Ow!" she yelped. The stretchy man had grown fangs, and it bit Violet's fingers, but she didn't let go.

Mia pulled out the tin, and they stuffed the stretchy man inside with the other two.

"Horrible creature!" said Violet, shaking her

injured hand.

"Here, I can heal you," said Sita.

She touched Violet's hand and breathed in deeply. Before their eyes, the wound closed up. Violet smiled at Sita.

"So, there wasn't really a Shade following me? It was just an illusion?" Sita said.

"Yes, caused by that Shade," said Mia. "I think that Mrs. Crooks has somehow figured out that we're Star Friends, and she stuck those stretchy men to the sparklers before Aunt Carol gave them to us."

"But why?" said Sita.

"To distract us from following her!"

Sita frowned. "But she'd only just met us earlier that day."

"Well," said Mia, realizing that Sita was right, "maybe she knew we were Star Friends before she actually met us. That could be why she was so horrible to us in the clearing."

"Okay, but if she was putting Shades into

the stretchy men, why does she have all those gnomes?" Sita said.

Mia frowned. She couldn't think of an answer to that.

"Right now, we don't have time to figure this out," said Violet. "We have to help Lexi." She held out her hands. "Come on, let's shadow-travel!"

When they arrived in Lexi's room, everything was neat and tidy, like always, but Lexi was sitting on the floor with a letter in her hands, in tears. Juniper was smoothing her hair with his little paws. "Don't cry, please don't cry," he was begging.

"But I failed my piano exam." Lexi picked up another letter from the floor beside her. "And the math challenge."

"Hi, Lexi!" Mia said.

Lexi almost jumped out of her skin.

The girls called their animals' names, and they appeared, too.

Lexi stared. "Why are you all here? What's going on?" she whispered.

"Well, it's like this—" Violet began.

"Shh!" Lexi said hastily. "Mom and Dad are downstairs!"

"We'll be quiet," promised Mia in a quiet voice.

"Well, we'll try," said Sita, looking around anxiously.

"So why did you come?" demanded Lexi. "Was it because you heard about my exam results?" She held up the letters. "I failed math and piano."

"I don't think you did." Mia really hoped she was right. She let magic tingle through her. To her relief, the letters in Lexi's hand started to glow with a shining outline. "They're just an illusion!" She touched them. "You're not real," she said.

When the letters vanished, Lexi gasped.
"What happened?"

"A Fear Shade made those letters appear,"
Mia explained. "It made you believe your fears
were coming true. You haven't failed your
exams."

Lexi stared. "Really? Oh my goodness, I've
been so worried. So it was all a Shade?"

The others nodded.

There was a slight rustling noise, and
Bracken and Sorrel swung around to see a
stretchy man creeping across Lexi's desk.

"There it is!" said Bracken.

The stretchy man started to run, but in a flash, Juniper had jumped onto the table and grabbed him in his paws. "You're going nowhere!" Juniper exclaimed.

"Except for back to the shadows!" added Violet.

The stretchy man struggled in Juniper's grasp.

Mia took the tin out of her bag and opened it just enough to get the little man in and then slammed it shut. "Got him!" She looked at the others. "Now what do we do?"

"We need to send them back to the shadows," said Lexi.

"How exactly do you plan to do that?" said Sorrel. "Do I have to remind you that Violet must be looking a Shade in the eyes to be able to command it? That may be a problem."

Mia bit her lip. Sorrel was right. The stretchy men moved so fast when they were free—and there were four of them. How could Violet

hope to be able to look them all in the eye at the same time?

"Maybe we should try sending them back one at a time," said Lexi. "If we open the tin and take one out, Violet could try and command it."

The lid on the tin shifted upward slightly as the stretchy men inside tried to get out.

"We'd better be quick!" said Sita. "This could go horribly wrong if they all escape."

"Okay, let's open the lid," said Lexi. "Violet, get ready."

"Remember, they bite," warned Mia. "Here goes!" She loosened one corner of the lid of the tin.

WHAM! The lid exploded off the tin, and the stretchy men leaped out.

Sita screamed, and Mia ducked as one jumped over her shoulder. Violet staggered back as another launched itself straight at her face with its claws out. Luckily Lexi saw what

was happening and, using her super-speed, she sprang in front of Violet and batted it away just in time. It flew through the air and landed on the floor.

"Thank you!" Violet gasped.

The animals sprang into action, trying to pounce and grab, but the stretchy men seemed to be everywhere. One of them reached the door, and Mia realized the man was planning on squeezing underneath it.

"Stop it!" she cried.

Mia and Violet both threw themselves forward, but even as Mia felt her fingers close around it, it seemed to slip out from between her fingers.

"It's escaping!" cried Violet.

"Freeze! Everyone, freeze!" exclaimed Sita.

All of a sudden, Mia found that she couldn't move. What was going on? She could see that everyone—her friends, the animals, and even the stretchy men—were frozen in their tracks.

"Oh," Sita said faintly, looking around the
room. "I didn't think it would work that well."

Mia's thoughts raced. How had Sita made
everyone do as she said?

Sita took a trembling breath. "Okay, listen
to me. Mia, Lexi, and Violet, I want you all to
unfreeze. Bracken, Willow, Juniper, and Sorrel,
too. *Unfreeze!*"

It was as if a magic wand had been waved.
Suddenly, Mia found she could move again.

"What's going on?" Lexi said, staring at Sita,
who was standing in the middle of the room

looking sheepish.

Willow trotted over to Sita. "Your magic, Sita," she said softly. "It's just as we thought."

"I know," said Sita in a small voice. "I'm not sure I like it." Willow nuzzled her.

"What are you talking about?" demanded Violet.

"Yes, enough of talking in riddles. Will one of you please explain what just happened?" said Sorrel sharply.

Sita put her hand on Willow's head. "Um … we were planning to tell you all about it, but then everything started going wrong, and I couldn't focus on anything other than the Shade I thought was following me. You know we all thought my magic had to do with healing and soothing people?"

They all nodded.

"Well, it *is* about healing, but I think that the soothing part isn't quite what it seems. People do calm down when I tell them to…." She glanced at Willow for help.

"But it's because Sita's magic lets her command others," explained Willow. "If she tells them to do something, they have to do it. People, animals, Shades."

Mia looked around at the four little stretchy men still frozen in position—one halfway under the door, one crouching down, one bending over, one on his tummy. Their eyes were rolling furiously as they fought against the magic, but they couldn't move.

"That's awesome," breathed Lexi.

"And scary," said Sita, with a slight shake to her voice.

"Sita, you must be the really powerful one the Shade told us about!" Mia realized.

"But I don't want to be," Sita said.

"I don't think you have a choice," said Bracken.

Sorrel gazed at Sita. "You will be in danger. A person using dark magic would do anything for your kind of power."

"Oh," Sita whispered.

Lexi picked up a frozen stretchy man that was lying near to her. "Look, let's talk about this more after we've sent these Shades back to the shadows." She looked at Willow. "Can Sita do that?"

"No, Sita can command them in this world, but only a Spirit Speaker like Violet can send spirits between worlds," Willow said.

"But what Sita can do is command the Shades to look Violet in the eyes," said Sorrel.

She picked up a stretchy man in her mouth and held it up to Violet.

Lexi nudged Sita. "Go on then. Do your commanding thing."

"Stretchy men, I … um … want you all to look at Violet," said Sita.

Sure enough, all four stretchy men reluctantly looked at Violet.

"Go back to the shadows where you

belong!" Violet said. The Shades shivered and shook and then, with a last wide-eyed look, they fell still.

"It worked!" said Sita in delight.

The animals bounded around the room.

"Great job, Sita," said Willow.

"That was amazing!" yapped Bracken.

"Shh!" said Lexi, glancing toward the door.

"You did exceptionally well," Sorrel purred to Violet.

"The Shades are really gone," Violet said in a low voice. "It's over!"

Mia shook her head. "No, it's not."

"What do you mean?" said Violet.

Mia took a deep breath. "We've still got Mrs. Crooks to deal with."

12
The Real Mrs. Crooks

Violet grabbed Mia's hand. "Time to shadow-travel to Mrs. Crooks's house!"

"No," said Sita quickly. "Not now. It's late. Imagine what will happen if our parents come looking for us and we're not in our bedrooms! They might even have discovered we're missing already."

Mia hesitated, but Sita was right. "Okay, we'll go over to her house tomorrow after school then."

The others all nodded.

They said good-bye to Lexi and all their
Star Animals, and then Violet shadow-
traveled with Sita and Mia back to Sita's
house. Leaving Sita there, they went on
to Violet's. As they arrived in the shadows
beside her closet, there was a knock on her
bedroom door.

"Do you two need anything?" Violet's mom
said, opening the door and looking in. "How's
the homework going?"

"Fine. We just finished, Mom," said Violet,
smoothing down her hair.

Mia nodded. "I'll call my dad and ask him to
come and get me."

"Don't worry. I can bring you home,"
Violet's mom said.

Mia and Violet shared a look of relief—that
had been close. What would have happened if
they hadn't gotten back in time? Shadow-travel
was amazing but very risky.

As Mrs. Cooper drove Mia and Violet past

Mrs. Crooks's house on the way back to her house, Mia wondered what Mrs. Crooks was doing. All the lights were off in the house. Was she out in the woods gathering plants and herbs to do more dark magic? Mia shivered. How could they possibly stop her?

Sita, Mia realized, thinking of Sita's new power. She'd be able to command Mrs. Crooks. *Tomorrow*, Mia thought. *Tomorrow we'll stop the dark magic once and for all.*

✦ ✦ ✦

After school the next day, the girls asked if they could go for a walk and then have dinner at Mia's house. To their relief, all their parents agreed. They headed to Mrs. Crooks's house and stopped on the street. "Okay," said Violet. "As soon as she opens the door, you've got to use your magic, Sita, and make her ask us in. Then, once we're in, you need to command her to tell us about the dark magic she's been doing."

"I'm scared," said Sita, her eyes wide.

Mia squeezed her hand. "Don't be. We'll all be with you."

They started to walk down the driveway, but before they could reach the door, Mrs. Crooks came out. "What are you girls doing here?" she demanded.

Her dog ran out and started barking at them. It snapped at Sita's ankles, making her squeal and back away.

"Jack! Stop that! Come here!" called Mrs. Crooks. "You girls, go away!" she said angrily. "You heard me! Go away! Stop upsetting my dog!"

With all the noise and confusion, Sita didn't have a chance to try and use her magic on Mrs. Crooks.

"We're not upsetting him!" Violet shouted.

"What's going on here?" Hearing a familiar voice, Mia swung around and saw Mary from the Copper Kettle bakery. "Jenny, what's happening?

Jack, come here! Stop making all that noise."

To Mia's surprise, the dog stopped barking and ran over to Mary, greeting her with a wagging tail. Mary took hold of his collar.

"These children are bothering him, Mary," said Mrs. Crooks angrily. "Hanging around on my driveway. Trying to upset him."

Mary shook her head. "These girls are sweet. They wouldn't do that—they all adore animals."

Mrs. Crooks harrumphed.

"Girls, I'm sorry about this. Please excuse my sister," Mary said to them. "She's not very fond of young people."

Mia stared. Mary and horrible Mrs. Crooks were sisters? Yes, now that she looked, she could see similarities between them, but Mary's face was open and smiling, whereas Mrs. Crooks's was closed and suspicious.

"Calm down, Jenny. I promise you, these girls wouldn't ever hurt an animal. Would you, girls?" Mary went on.

"Never! We all love animals," said Violet.

"We really do," Lexi said, holding her hand out to the dog. He growled.

"I'm sorry, Lexi," Mary said. "Jack's not very good with young people. He was a stray who was badly treated by some teenagers once. That's why he only has one ear. He came into the vet's where Jenny used to work. She helped get him better and then adopted him."

"Oh," Mia said slowly.

"Jenny's working at the new wildlife sanctuary," Mary went on.

Mia's mind spun as she tried to match Mrs. Crooks the conjurer of Shades with Mrs. Crooks the animal lover whom Mary was telling her about.

"We have badgers and foxes and rabbits," said Mrs. Crooks, slightly gruffly. "And squirrels and weasels. Some of the animals we keep away from visitors—those who aren't too badly injured and who are going to be released back into the wild. The ones that need a lot of care become too trusting of people, so they have to stay at the sanctuary. They're often injured because of young people—" she gave them a stern look—"leaving litter in the woods. But Mary's right. If you like wildlife, you should come and visit."

Mary smiled. "Maybe today they could take a quick look in your shed, Jenny."

Shed! Mia saw the others' eyes all widen.

Mrs. Crooks nodded. "I don't see why not. Provided you're quiet and don't touch anything,"

"What's in the shed?" Violet ventured.

A rare smile lifted the corners of Mrs. Crooks's mouth. "Animals," she said. "Would you like to see?"

The girls exchanged looks. For a moment, Mia wondered if Mary and Mrs. Crooks were doing dark magic together. She wanted to see inside the shed—after all, it was what they had come here for—but was it an elaborate trap?

"Um … our parents probably wouldn't like us to come in without getting permission first," Lexi said slowly.

"Of course," said Mary. "Good girls. That's very sensible of you."

Just then a car pulled up. "Hi, girls," said Mia's mom, putting down the window. "Is everything okay?"

"Everything's fine," said Mary.

"Mom—" Mia felt a little nervous, but she knew she had to get to the bottom of this—"Mrs. Crooks just asked us if we want to see inside her shed. Is it okay if we do?"

"Jenny has some animals in there," said Mary.

"Sure," said Mrs. Greene. "I'm just popping over to the store to get some cheese and pepperoni. I can pick you up on the way back. Dad made some pizza dough, so you can make your own pizzas for dinner."

The girls nodded and followed Mrs. Crooks into the house. There were pictures of animals on the walls, and the kitchen smelled of baking bread.

"Come this way," said Mrs. Crooks.

As the girls stepped through the back door into the yard, they all gasped. There were pottery gnomes everywhere! They all had jolly faces—some were fishing in a pond, others pushing wheelbarrows or carrying baskets.

There were also pottery toadstools and animals. "Oh ... wow!" said Mia.

"I collect yard ornaments," Mrs. Crooks said, looking happy at their reaction.

Mary smiled. "Do you like them, girls?"

"Yes," said Mia, looking around in astonishment. Sorrel had been right— there were a lot of gnomes ... but they weren't sinister. The yard was like a fairy-tale forest scene.

"I'd love a yard like this," said Sita.

"Jenny's been collecting since we were children," said Mary. "Some of them are really valuable now."

"Is that why you have such a high fence?" Lexi asked.

Mrs. Crooks nodded. "I had a couple of pieces stolen from the yard at my old house, so I had the fence put up when I moved in here." She headed up a winding gravel path. Reaching the shed, she put her finger to her lips and opened the door. It was dark inside, and the air was filled with the scent of hay and animals. There were cages, just as Mia had seen in her mirror. Some were empty, but others had animals in them—the girls could see that some of them had bandages or wounds that had been recently stitched up. The animals blinked warily at the girls in the dim light.

"There's a squirrel," whispered Lexi.

"And rabbits and a baby badger," added Violet.

"These animals will all be released into the wild again soon," Mrs. Crooks said in a low voice. "When I find an injured animal, I bring it here first. The vet comes to assess the animals and takes the ones that need a lot of veterinary help to the sanctuary." Her face softened as she looked at them. "They're my little beauties, and I try my best to help them so they can be set free."

Mia swallowed. She suddenly realized that they'd been so, so wrong about Mrs. Crooks. She wasn't the person doing dark magic. She was just an elderly woman who loved animals.

"Jenny goes out into the woods looking for injured animals," said Mary.

"I'm sorry if I've been bad-tempered with you, girls," Mrs. Crooks said gruffly. "So many young people don't think about how their actions affect the wildlife—they leave litter, set off fireworks that scare animals, disturb their nests and habitats."

"We'd never do that," Sita said.

"I realize that now," said Mrs. Crooks. "I'm sorry. I shouldn't have been so quick to judge."

She pulled the door shut, and the girls
followed her back up the path. As Mia saw the
gnomes again, she thought of something. "Mrs.
Crooks, did you give a gnome to the Eastons?"

"The Eastons? No, I don't know who you
mean," said Mrs. Crooks.

"They live on Brook Street. There's a big
trampoline in the front yard," said Mia, feeling
puzzled. She'd definitely seen Mrs. Crooks with
the Wish Gnome—so either the magic had
been wrong, or Mrs. Crooks was lying.

Mrs. Crooks's face cleared. "Oh, I know that
house. They do have a gnome in the yard, don't
they? I picked it up to look at it a week or so
ago when I was passing by. I couldn't resist. It
was a nice specimen, and yes, just like some of
mine, but no, I didn't give it to them."

Mia's breath left her in a rush. So the image
she'd seen had been Mrs. Crooks admiring the
gnome, but she hadn't been the person who
had given it to Paige's mom. "Thank you for

showing us the animals," Mia said.

"Yes, and we'll come and visit the sanctuary soon," said Sita.

"Make sure you come and find me when you do," said Mrs. Crooks, leading them through the house and letting them out the front door. "And I'll give you a guided tour."

They said good-bye, and she shut the door.

The girls looked at each other. "Okay, so maybe we got it wrong," said Lexi slowly.

They all nodded. "We really did," said Mia.

"But if Mrs. Crooks didn't conjure the Shades, who did?" said Sita.

"I still think it must be someone who knows we're Star Friends," said Violet.

Mia lifted her chin. "Well, they can try all they like, but they're not going to stop us—we're going to find out who's using dark magic."

"They've got no chance against us," Lexi said. "Not with Sita's power."

"It's *all* of our powers that will stop them," said Sita.

Lexi smiled. "The important thing is that we did it—we sent all four Shades back to the shadows."

"And next we'll deal with whoever it is using dark magic," said Mia. "Won't we?" She held her up hand.

"Definitely," they all chorused, high-fiving her.

Just then, there was a beep of a car horn, and Mrs. Greene pulled up alongside them. "Ready for some homemade pizza, girls?" she asked, and the friends all piled into the car.

Mia looked out the window at the pretty town of Westport as they drove back to her house. Together with her friends and their Star Animals, they would keep everyone safe and happy. Nothing—and no one—was going to stop them.

Star Friends

DARK TRICKS

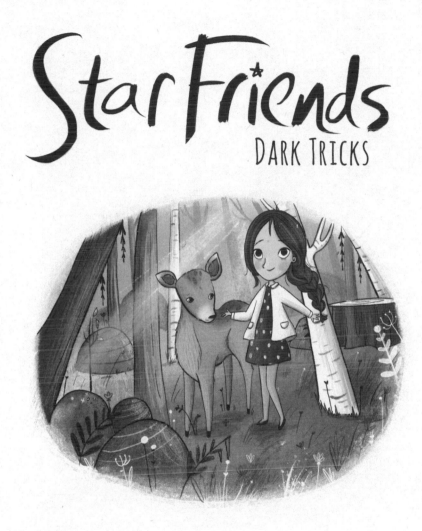

To Tabitha Fox-Jalland, who would probably have
at least ten Star Animals (including a Star Sheep)
following her around!—L.C.

To Katherine—L.F.

Contents

1
IN THE STAR WORLD

A waterfall of stars fell into a beautiful pool. A snowy owl and a silver wolf stood beside it, watching intently as an image appeared in the water—a gray-haired lady holding a glittering black stone.

"I don't like this, Hunter," the wolf said. "She is full of bitterness and jealousy, and she is planning on harming the new Star Friends."

The owl nodded in concern and swept his wing across the surface of the water. The image of the elderly lady dissolved and reformed, this

time showing four ten-year-old girls chatting in a bedroom. There were four animals with them—a fox, a wildcat, a young deer, and a red squirrel. Each of the animals had unusual indigo eyes— they were animals from the Star World.

The wolf gazed at one of the girls—she had shoulder-length, dark blond hair and determined eyes. The fox was cuddled up next to her, resting his head on her shoulder. "Mia looks so much like her grandmother," the wolf said.

"I hope she has her grandmother's courage and cleverness," said the owl gravely. "These four girls and their Star Animals will have to be very brave if they are going to stop the one using dark magic. They will have to trust their instincts, their friendship—but most of all, their hearts...."

2
A LITTLE MORNING MAGIC

Mia Greene sat cross-legged on her bed. Magic tingled through her, making her feel as if every inch of her skin was sparkling. Her Star Animal, Bracken the fox, sat beside her, but her eyes were fixed on the small mirror in her hands. Through her bedroom door, she could hear her older sister, Cleo, shouting to their mom that she couldn't find her favorite skirt.

"Show me where Cleo's favorite skirt is," Mia whispered.

The surface of the mirror shimmered, and

a picture appeared. It showed a red skirt lying in a pile underneath the dresser in Cleo's bedroom.

"Found it!" Mia said in delight. When she had first started learning how to do magic, it would take her quite a while to connect with the magic current, but now she could do it almost instantly.

Mia had been able to use magic ever since Bracken and some other animals from the Star World had appeared to find Star Friends. Only those who truly believed in magic could hear the Star Animals speaking. Together, a Star Friend and their Star Animal would use the magical current that flowed between the two worlds to help people. Each Star Friend had different magical abilities, and when they used magic for good, it strengthened the current.

Bracken nuzzled Mia, his soft fur tickling her skin. "You're getting so good at using magic!"

he said.

Mia breathed in his familiar sweet scent—
the smell of grass in the woods on a warm
autumn day. "Good. I need to be strong if we
want to stop whoever is using dark magic. We
all need to be."

Mia's three best friends, Lexi, Sita, and
Violet, were also Star Friends. Together they
had discovered that someone nearby was using
dark magic to conjure Shades, and that this
was weakening the magical current. Shades
were evil spirits who brought misery and
unhappiness into people's lives, and Star Friends
could use their magic to send them back to the
shadows.

"We'll find whoever is conjuring Shades and
stop them," Bracken declared. "Are we meeting
up with the others today?"

"Yes, we're going to Violet's house later this
morning. I thought I'd stop by Aunt Carol's on
the way."

Aunt Carol had been friends with Mia's grandmother before she had died. She was the only adult Mia knew who could do magic—she wasn't a Star Friend like Mia, but used crystals and stones.

Mia heard her sister shouting on the landing again. "Oops, I still haven't told Cleo where her skirt is."

Bracken disappeared in a shimmer of starlight as Mia opened the bedroom door. None of Mia's family knew about him—the Star World had to be kept secret from people who didn't believe in magic.

Cleo was standing at the top of the stairs shouting, "I've looked *everywhere*!"

"Wear something else, then," her mom said.

"But I want to wear my skirt!"

Mia went into Cleo's messy bedroom and hurried over to the dresser. She crouched down. Just then, Cleo came into the room. "What are you doing in here?" she asked.

"I thought I'd help you look for your skirt," said Mia. "Is this it?" She pulled the red skirt out from under the dresser.

"Yes!" Cleo gasped. She frowned. "Did you put it there?"

"No!" Mia protested. "Just a lucky guess."

Their mom appeared in the doorway. "Cleo, this room is a mess. It's no wonder you can't find anything!"

"Mom! Mia found my skirt!" Cleo said. "You keep doing this—finding things that are lost. How do you do it?"

Mia hid her smile. If only Cleo knew the truth! "I guess I'm just good at finding things."

"I think you're psychic," said Cleo, staring at her. "You should start a social media channel!"

Mia laughed it off but thought that maybe she should be a little more careful about how she used her magic from now on.

"Cleo, I hardly think Mia's psychic," Mom said, smiling. "I think you're just very bad at looking. Now get changed quickly, and I'll drop you off at your friend's house. What are you going to do this morning, Mia?" she asked as they both left Cleo's room.

"I'm meeting the others at Violet's house. Is it okay if I go to Aunt Carol's on the way?"

"Of course," Mom said. "Aunt Carol always loves to see you. Tell her I'll stop by for a cup of tea soon."

"Okay," Mia said, and she hurried down the stairs.

3
A VISIT WITH AUNT CAROL

As Mia rode her bike through the streets of
Westport, the coastal town where she lived, the
frosty November air stung her cheeks. Autumn
had definitely turned to winter now—the
branches of the trees were almost bare, and
there was a thin coating of frost on the grass.

As she rode along, the locals she passed
smiled at her and said hello. It was hard to
believe that someone in town wanted to use
magic to hurt people. But Mia and her friends
had dealt with a Mirror Shade who had been

making Cleo jealous of her best friend and a Wish Shade trapped inside a garden gnome who had made a little girl's wish come true in horrible ways. Then, last week, they had faced Fear Shades that were hidden in four little yellow stretchy men. The Fear Shades had made it seem as if people's worst fears were coming true. Luckily, Mia and her friends had realized what was going on and had managed to send them back to the shadows, too.

We have to find out who is causing all this trouble, Mia thought.

Mia got off her bike and leaned it against the wall in front of Aunt Carol's house. She glanced toward the house on the right, feeling guilty as she remembered how she and the others had suspected that the eccentric elderly lady who lived there—Mrs. Crooks—was the person doing dark magic. The Wish Shade in the gnome had told them that the person who had conjured him was a woman, and when they had first met Mrs. Crooks, they had suspected her right away. She liked to go out into the woods at night, she was very grumpy, she had a bunch of garden gnomes, and Sorrel had even smelled Shades near her yard. But it had turned out that Mrs. Crooks was just a harmless elderly lady who didn't like children very much and loved to collect garden ornaments and rescue injured animals in the woods.

Looking at the two gnomes sitting on either side of Mrs. Crooks' front door, Mia wondered who had put the Wish Shade in the gnome that had been given to Paige.

Aunt Carol opened her front door and beamed. "Hello, Mia. I wasn't expecting you."

"I was on my way to Violet's, and I thought I'd stop in," said Mia.

"How lovely! I've just made some of my chocolate cookies—the ones I know you like."

Mia took off her shoes in the hall and went through to the familiar living room, with its displays of polished stones and crystals decorating the shelves. She spotted an open cardboard box filled with cute knitted Christmas decorations on the coffee table— there were penguins, snowmen, and reindeer, all with beautiful sparkling eyes made out of tiny black crystals.

"These are beautiful," Mia said to Aunt Carol.

"Thank you, Mia. I've been making them to sell at the Christmas fair this weekend. You are going to come, aren't you?"

The Christmas fair was held every November

in the town hall. There were homemade cakes for sale as well as Christmas decorations, cards, and gifts. Mia's Grandma Anne had organized it when she was alive, and Mia had been to it every year for as long as she could remember.

"Yes, I'll be there," Mia said.

"It'll be strange without your grandma this year," said Aunt Carol. "But we'll make sure it's a really special one. The town will have the fair it deserves! Now come into the kitchen and have a cookie."

They went into the kitchen at the back of the house and sat down at the table. "Have you and your friends gotten any closer to solving the mystery of who is conjuring the Shades?" Aunt Carol asked as Mia helped herself to a cookie. "When I last saw you, you said that you thought it might be Mrs. Crooks. I've been keeping an eye on her, and she does act suspiciously—going out into the woods at all times of the day and night and—"

"Oh, it's okay, Aunt Carol," Mia put in. "It's not Mrs. Crooks. We still don't know who it is, though. But we think that whoever it is put stretchy men with Shades trapped inside them onto the boxes of sparklers you gave us."

Aunt Carol looked shocked. "Those little stretchy men had Shades in them?"

Mia nodded and gave a shiver. "Yes. Fear Shades. They were horrible."

"But you've sent them back to the Shadows? How did you manage that?" said Aunt Carol, intrigued.

"It was Violet and Sita, really," said Mia. "Violet's a Spirit Speaker, so she sent them back to the shadows, and Sita discovered she has this amazing ability—she can use her magic to command people and spirits to do what she wants. If she orders you to do something, you have to do it."

"Really?" Aunt Carol breathed. "That's a very rare ability. Your grandmother had it, too."

Mia nodded. She'd used her magic to
look back into the past and had seen her
grandmother using the same powers as Sita.
Star Friends all had different magical abilities—
Mia could use the magic current to see into
the past and future and to see things that were
happening elsewhere. Lexi could become very
agile and fast, and Violet could travel from place
to place using shadows and command Shades
to return to the shadows as well as casting
illusions. At first, they'd thought that Sita's
magic just allowed her to heal and soothe. But
then, last week, she had discovered she could
command people and spirits, too. "I don't think
Sita likes being so powerful."

"Well, if she wants to talk about it, she's
always welcome here," said Aunt Carol. "I
might be able to help."

"Thanks, I'll tell her," Mia said. Suddenly, she
remembered something she'd been meaning to
ask. "Where did you get those sparklers from,

Aunt Carol? The ones that the stretchy men were attached to?"

"From the garden center," said Aunt Carol. "If I'd known there were Shades in those stretchy men, I never would have given them to you. I wonder who put them there. Have you tried using the Seeing Stone to find out?"

"No, but I have been using it to look at other things," said Mia. Aunt Carol had given Mia a pale pink Seeing Stone to help her look into the past. Although Mia could use Star Magic to do that, she found it much easier with the Seeing Stone. "I've been looking into the past, to when you and Grandma Anne were younger. I've seen you doing magic together."

"I'm glad you've been using it." Aunt Carol smiled. "You're a natural with crystal magic as well as Star Magic."

Mia glowed proudly. "I'd better go," she said, checking the clock on the wall, "or the others will wonder where I am."

"Wait a minute." Aunt Carol hurried to the
living room and came back with four knitted
decorations. "Please give one to each of your
friends to say how sorry I am about those
stretchy men."

"Thank you," said Mia.

As she headed to the front door, she noticed
a large snow globe on the side table in the
hallway. She was surprised to see that it was
empty except for a thin layer of snow. "I've
never seen a snow globe without anything
inside it before," she said.

"It won't be empty for long. This is going to be a very special snow globe," said Aunt Carol.

"Why?" asked Mia curiously.

"Oh, you'll find out," Aunt Carol said, tapping her nose. "I just need to test it first." Mia opened her mouth, but Aunt Carol said, "Now don't ask any questions. Like I said, you'll find out soon enough."

Mia put on her coat and helmet and rode off as Aunt Carol waved from the doorway. What had Aunt Carol meant? *Maybe the snow globe is magic and she's going to put something special inside it as a present*, Mia thought excitedly.

Crossing the main road, she turned onto the road that led down to the beach. Seeing Lexi and Sita arriving at the driveway of Violet's house, Mia rode quickly to catch up with her friends.

4
A Star Friends Meeting

"Hi, Mia!" Lexi called, jumping off her bike. Her black curls stuck out from under her pink helmet. She pulled it off and readjusted the butterfly clip in her hair.

"Hello." Sita's gentle brown eyes sparkled as she whispered, "Are you ready to do magic?"

Mia grinned. "Always."

As Mia propped her bike against the fence, she accidentally brushed her hand against some nettles. "Ow!" she exclaimed.

"Let me look," said Sita.

Mia held out her hand. Sita touched the nettle rash and concentrated for a second. The pain and tingling faded, and the bumps disappeared.

"That's awesome," said Mia, inspecting her hand. "Thank you."

Sita sighed happily. "I love using magic to heal."

The door opened, and Violet looked out. "I thought I heard you. Come in!" They all hurried upstairs to Violet's bedroom. As soon as the door was shut behind them, they called their Star Animals' names.

"Bracken!"

"Juniper!"

"Sorrel!"

"Willow!"

In a wave of starry light, the four animals appeared. Bracken put his paws up on Mia's knees and licked her face. Juniper, a red squirrel with a bushy tail, jumped onto the dressing table and then from there onto Lexi's shoulder. He tickled Lexi's cheek with his little paws, making her giggle and squirm. Willow, a deer with a coat the color of a chestnut, nuzzled Sita's hands, and Sorrel the wildcat wound through Violet's legs purring happily, her tail high in the air.

When the greetings were over, they all sat down on the rug, the animals happily cuddling up to their Star Friends.

"Has anyone used their magic since yesterday?" Mia asked.

"I have," said Lexi. "I was walking home from my piano lesson, and I saw a cat about to run into the road. I used my magic to move really quickly, and I grabbed it and took it to safety."

"That's amazing!" said Sita. "I used my magic to heal my baby brother after he bumped his head on the coffee table."

"Cool!" said Mia.

"Have you used your powers to command people yet?" Violet asked Sita.

Sita shook her head.

"I'd use that power if I had it," said Violet longingly.

"Why haven't you?" Lexi asked.

"I just haven't," Sita muttered.

Willow spoke up. "What have you used your magic for, Violet?"

"Violet's been wonderful," said Sorrel smugly. "Tell them, Violet."

"I used my magic to shadow-travel to the park. We'd been playing there, and my little cousin had left her cuddly monkey. I went to find it and bring it back," said Violet.

"Very clever," Sorrel said approvingly.

Mia caught sight of Lexi rolling her eyes. Sorrel always acted as if Violet was better than the rest of them. Mia didn't mind, but it irritated Lexi.

"How about you, Mia?" said Sita.

"Well, I used my magic to find Cleo's skirt this morning," Mia said.

"That's all you've done?" Sorrel said, not sounding impressed.

Bracken stiffened. "It might have been a small thing, but it was still a good deed." He rubbed his head against Mia's leg.

Sorrel gave him a cool look. "Not like Violet's."

"I bet Cleo was happy, though," said Violet quickly.

"Yes, but the trouble is, now she thinks I'm some kind of weird psychic," said Mia.

"Mystic Mia," Lexi said, grinning. "You could use your powers to tell people's fortunes and earn a lot of money."

Sorrel sniffed. "Do I need to remind you that magic should only be used for good?"

"Mia would be doing good—she'd be helping us!" said Lexi.

Juniper chattered as if he was laughing, and Bracken yapped playfully, but Sorrel flicked her tail around her paws, a disapproving look on her face.

"Have you been practicing looking into the past, Mia?" Sita asked.

"A bit," said Mia. She didn't want to admit she'd been using the Seeing Stone. Bracken

thought she should only use Star Magic, and
she had a feeling that the other Star Animals—
especially Sorrel—would agree with him.
"Oh, I just remembered something," she said,
changing the subject. "I stopped by to see
Aunt Carol on the way here, and she gave me
Christmas decorations for all of us." She took
them from her pocket and handed them out,
keeping a snowman for herself.

"Cute!" said Lexi, looking at her reindeer.

Sita looked at the penguin Mia had given
her. "My grandma would love this. She adores
penguins. I'll give it to her."

"Wait!" Sorrel hissed suddenly, her fur standing up. "Those decorations could have Shades in them." She pounced on the knitted snowman Violet was holding and sniffed it suspiciously. "They're safe," she said grudgingly.

"Of course they are," said Mia as Violet put the snowman on her desk. "Aunt Carol's decorations wouldn't be bad. She only uses magic for good."

"She did give you the stretchy men," Sorrel reminded them.

"But she hadn't even noticed them. She picked the boxes up from the garden center!" Mia protested.

Violet looked thoughtful. "Maybe if we go there, we might find out something about them."

"How do we get there, though?" said Lexi. "We could ask one of our parents to take us…."

"I could shadow-travel us!" exclaimed Violet. Recently, she had found out that she could take other people with her when she was shadow-traveling. She jumped to her feet. "Come on!"

"Wait! What if your mom comes in and sees that we're all gone?" said Sita.

"She'll be really worried," Willow added.

"I don't mind staying," offered Sita. "If your mom does pop in, I can say the rest of you went outside or something."

"I'll stay, too," Mia said. She wanted a chance to talk to Sita about her new powers. "I will use my magic so Sita and I can watch what you're doing," she told Lexi and Violet.

Violet looked at Lexi. "Okay, I guess it's you and me, then." She and Lexi had never been very good friends—they were both clever and very competitive—and they rarely did anything just the two of them.

"I guess it is," said Lexi, giving Mia a slightly panicked look.

Violet walked to a patch of shadows in the corner of the room and held out her hand. Lexi joined her—then they and their Star Animals disappeared.

5
GATHERING CLUES

Mia and Sita stared at the empty shadows.

"I hope they're okay," said Sita anxiously. "What if someone notices them suddenly appearing in the garden center?"

Mia pulled a small mirror out of her pocket—she always carried it with her in case she wanted to do magic. She said Lexi and Violet's names, and she saw in the mirror her friends stepping out of the shadows beside a display of lawnmowers. Luckily, no one seemed to notice. "They just got there. They seem okay.

I'll check again in a minute." She lowered the mirror. "So how are you?"

"Me? All right." Sita shrugged, tucking a strand of hair behind her ear. "Why?"

"I just wondered how you were feeling about being able to command people," Mia said.

Willow nudged Sita encouragingly. "Talk to Mia. Tell her."

"Well, to be honest, I… I don't like it," Sita muttered. "I'm not even sure if it's real. I mean, it could just have been a fluke when I stopped those stretchy men."

"It wasn't," Bracken said.

"No way," said Mia, shaking her head. "You told us to freeze, and none of us could move until you freed us. Your power's real."

"But it can't be!" Sita said desperately. "I can't even decide what clothes to wear in the morning or how to do my hair. I *can't* be the powerful one."

"But you are," Bracken told her. "And that's good, isn't it?"

"No. It's a mistake," Sita said. Her eyes filled with tears.

"Hey, don't stress about it," Mia said, squeezing Sita's hand. "Aunt Carol suggested that you stop over and see her if you want to talk. My grandma had the same power as you, and Aunt Carol can help you." Not wanting to upset Sita anymore, she changed the subject. "Should we check on the others again?"

This time, when Mia picked up the mirror, she saw Lexi and Violet standing by a display of gnomes. "They're by some garden gnomes!" she exclaimed. "They look just like the one the Wish Shade was in. Maybe he came from that garden center, just like the stretchy men!" Letting everything else fade away, she focused on the picture and heard Violet speak.

"Let's ask about them," she was
whispering to Lexi. "Then
we'll see if we can find
out more about the
stretchy men later."
She headed over
to a nearby store
assistant.

"Excuse me,
how much are the
gnomes?" Violet asked
politely.

The lady smiled. "They're
all different prices. The price tags are
underneath them. They're sweet, aren't they?"

Violet nodded. "Have they just arrived, or
have you had them for a while?"

"They came in a few months ago now."

"I think my grandma's friend might have
bought one," said Lexi, joining Violet. "It was a
gnome with a four-leaf clover on his hat. Does

that sound familiar?"

"Oh, yes! He was very cute," said the assistant. "He had a message on the base. *Make a Wish*, I think it said."

Lexi nodded fast. "That's the one."

"Do you remember when he was sold?" Violet asked eagerly.

The assistant nodded. "I do. It was about a month ago—and I remember the lady who bought him. She comes in quite a lot. She lives in Westport. Cheerful lady, small with gray hair and very blue eyes."

Mia's heart thumped. They had a description of the person who had bought the gnome!

"What's your grandma's friend's name?" the assistant asked

"Umm, she's…." Lexi gave Violet a panicked look. "She's…."

"Oh, my phone!" said Violet, pulling her phone out of her pocket. "It's my mom," she said to the assistant apologetically. "She's

probably wondering where we are. Thanks for your help." She held up the phone to her ear. "Hi, Mom," she said, pretending to answer a call as she dragged Lexi away around the side of a display of toys. "Yes, we're coming in just a minute."

Lexi squeaked and pointed at a shelf where there was a big box of stretchy men.

"Stretchy men!" Violet gasped. "I wonder if these have Shades in them, too. Sorrel, come here!" she whispered.

Mia caught her breath as she saw the wildcat appear. What if someone spotted her?

Violet pushed a stretchy man toward the cat. "Does this have a Shade in it?"

Sorrel sniffed. "No."

"Violet! Someone's coming. Quick!" Lexi hissed.

"Time to go!" said Violet, throwing the stretchy man back in the box.

Sorrel vanished, and Violet grabbed Lexi's

hand and pulled her into a patch of shadows.
They disappeared.

A second later, they were back in Violet's
bedroom, giggling and stumbling out of
the shadows beside Violet's closet. "Oh, my
goodness! Shadow-traveling is fun!" said Lexi.

"It really is, isn't it?" Violet gasped.

"What happened?" said Sita.

Lexi and Violet called Juniper and Sorrel's names, and the two animals appeared. Then they told the others what had happened.

"You both did exceptionally well," purred Sorrel.

Lexi grinned. "I didn't know what to say when the assistant asked me what my grandma's friend's name was. That was quick-thinking with the phone excuse, Violet."

Violet looked happy. "Thanks. Your idea of pretending your grandma's friend had bought a gnome was great, too. At least we know what the person who bought the gnome looks like now."

"She has gray hair and blue eyes, and she's small and from Westport," said Lexi.

They beamed at each other. Mia blinked. She didn't think she'd ever seen Lexi and Violet act like they were good friends before.

"There are quite a few older ladies in Westport like that," said Sita.

"I've got an idea," said Violet suddenly. "All the elderly ladies are bound to go to the Christmas fair this weekend. We can make a list of everyone there who matches that description. Then we can spy on them using Mia's magic and see if any of them acts suspiciously."

"That's a great plan!" said Mia. "I think we've got some real clues to go on now." She held out her hand. "Go us!"

"Go us!" echoed Sita, Violet, and Lexi, high-fiving each other.

6
MIA'S BAD MOOD

When Mia got home, she hung her snowman decoration on the handle of her closet door. As she called Bracken, she picked up the Seeing Stone from her desk. It glowed with a faint golden light. "I might try using the Seeing Stone to see Grandma Anne and Aunt Carol in the past," she told Bracken. She loved watching her grandmother when she was younger.

Bracken scratched his nose with a paw. "You're a Star Friend—you should use Star Magic, not Crystal Magic."

Mia reluctantly put the Seeing Stone into her pocket and sat down in front of the mirror on her desk. "Show me Grandma Anne when she was just learning about being a Star Friend."

The surface of the mirror began to swirl. She waited for it to form a clear image, but all she caught were brief pictures that appeared and then vanished—a young Grandma Anne cuddling her silver wolf…Grandma Anne with her hand on the wolf's back, smiling happily… Grandma Anne arguing with someone…. Mia squinted, trying to see who it was. It looked like it could be Aunt Carol, but before Mia could decide, the image flickered and was replaced by Grandma Anne healing a horse's leg.

"What can you see?" Bracken asked.

"Just a lot of different images flashing by," said Mia in frustration. "My magic is not working correctly."

Bracken looked surprised. "It was working fine earlier. Try looking at something that's happening now."

Mia looked into the mirror again. "Show me … Aunt Carol."

The surface swirled again, and she caught a glimpse of Aunt Carol holding the snow globe. She was smiling … but then the image swirled away.

"Aunt Carol," Mia said again, but nothing happened. "I can't even look into the present right now!" Mia gave Bracken a confused glance. "What's going on?"

Bracken looked puzzled. "It's very strange. Maybe you should take a break and try again later."

But that night, Mia still couldn't see anything clearly. In the end, she gave up and fell asleep with Bracken in her arms.

Mia woke up in a bad mood. It was a drizzly, gray morning, and on the way to school, Alex kept insisting that their mom stop the stroller so he could look at things.

"Cat!" he said. "Black cat."

"Yes, sweetie, that's right—it's a black cat," their mom said.

"Red car!" he said pointing to a shiny red car parked by the sidewalk. "Wanna see!"

Mrs. Greene pushed him over to it.

Mia felt irritation rise up inside her. "We're going to be late, Mom!"

"No, we're not," her mom said. "He just wants to take a look."

"He took a look!" said Mia.

Her mom frowned. "What's up with you this morning?"

"Nothing," Mia muttered.

"Dog!" said Alex next, pointing up ahead to where a brown and white spaniel was sniffing at some grass. The owner, Mrs. Patel, who had been a friend of Grandma Anne's, was talking to Aunt Carol.

Mia's mom went over to say hello.

"Hello, Mia. Hello, Alex," said Aunt Carol. "Off to school and playgroup?"

Mia forced herself to smile despite her bad mood. "Yep."

The dog licked Alex's outstretched hand and stuck her nose in his face. Alex giggled.

Mia crouched down to rub the dog's ears. Grandma Anne had sometimes taken care of Holly for the Patels when they went on vacation. "Hello, Holly dog," she said.

Holly bounced around Mia, her tail wagging really quickly.

"She's ready for her morning run in the woods," said Mrs. Patel. "Anytime you feel like dog-walking, Mia, feel free to come by!"

"I will," Mia promised.

She spotted Lexi, Sita, and Violet walking together a bit farther up the road. "I'll catch up with the others," she told her mom.

"All right. Have a good day!" her mom called.

Mia hurried after her friends. Sita looked lost in her thoughts, her hands playing with the ends of her blue and white polka-dot scarf, while Lexi and Violet were talking about the school math club, complaining about how the games and worksheets were always too easy. Mia felt a flicker of jealousy as she saw Lexi and Violet swap smiles, and she tried to push the feeling away. It was silly to be jealous—after all, she had been wanting Lexi and Violet to get along better for a long time.

They all greeted her. "Are we going to meet

after school so we can talk about stuff?" Violet said as they went onto the playground.

"Yeah, and do *stuff*," said Lexi, raising her eyebrows meaningfully. They tried not to mention magic when there were other people around, just in case anyone overheard.

"It's getting dark so early that we probably won't be allowed to go to the clearing in the woods," Violet said. "I'll ask if you can come to my house."

"That's a good idea," said Sita.

"I guess," said Mia a bit grumpily. She saw her friends give her surprised looks. "We went to Violet's last time."

"We can go to yours if you want," said Violet.

"No, it's okay," said Mia. She put down her bag and it fell over, spilling her books and lunch onto the wet ground.

"Rotten bag," she said angrily as the others helped her pick up her things, and she shoved everything back in.

The bell rang, and they made their way over
to line up in their class groups. Lexi and Sita
were together in one fifth-grade class, and Mia
and Violet were in the other.

"Are you okay?" Violet said, falling into step
with Mia. "You seem like you're in a bad mood."

"I'm fine," snapped Mia.

Violet stared at her. "There's no need to bite
my head off!"

As the day went on, Mia's bad mood faded.
At the end of school, their parents agreed that
they could all go over to Violet's house. They
were walking along the road when Mia spotted
a notice on a lamppost with a photograph
of a brown and white dog. She frowned and

hurried over. "Look! The Patels' dog is missing. I just saw her this morning!" She read the notice.

MISSING! PLEASE HELP!

Holly, our springer spaniel, ran off during her morning walk in the woods and hasn't been seen since. If anyone finds her or sees her, please contact us right away.

Call Kavita Patel—555-6693

"I wonder what happened to her," Mia said.

"I hope she hasn't been run over," said Sita anxiously.

"Maybe we can help find her," said Violet. "*With magic*," she mouthed, glancing back to where her dad was walking along talking to another dad.

They all nodded and hurried on down the road.

7
SOMETHING STRANGE

Violet dumped her bag on her desk next to her snowman decoration. "I've got to find a place to put this," she said, holding it up.

"You could hang it from your mirror," suggested Lexi.

"I gave mine to my grandma yesterday," said Sita. "She really liked it. She's going to buy some more at the Christmas fair."

Violet shut the door. "Okay, let's call the animals and see if we can help find Holly."

The others nodded. As soon as the Star

Animals appeared and heard about the missing dog, they agreed that the girls should try and find her using magic.

"Whose magic should we use?" Lexi asked.

"Well, I think it's obvious," said Violet. "We use Mia's magic to see where the dog is, and then you and I will shadow-travel there. If it's trapped somewhere, you can use your agility to rescue it. All set!"

Mia bit her lip. Her bad mood felt like it was creeping back. Why did Violet always think her plans were the best? "What about Sita?" she said. "That means she doesn't do anything."

"Maybe not everyone's magic is needed this time, Mia," Bracken said.

Annoyance flashed through Mia. "I think we should try and use everyone's magic."

"Why are you being so difficult?" Violet said.

"Yeah, Mia, what's your problem?" Lexi asked, frowning.

Mia glared. They were all ganging up on her!

"I don't mind if I'm not needed," Sita said quickly. "If the dog is injured or needs calming down, I can help in that way." She squeezed Mia's hand. "Thanks for being a good friend, though."

Mia felt the tension inside her slowly drain away. She started to sigh in relief, but then she realized what Sita was doing. "You're using your magic on me!" she exclaimed indignantly.

"No! Well, not my commanding magic. It's only my soothing, healing magic," Sita said. "I was just trying to help—you seemed tense."

"I'm not tense!" Mia exclaimed. She saw her

friends and their animals exchange surprised looks and added, "Oh, this is ridiculous! You can all find Holly without me!"

"Mia!" Bracken raced up and put his paws on her knees. "This isn't like you. What's the matter?"

Mia took a deep breath and crouched down, burying her face in his fur. Breathing in his familiar scent, she felt her anger begin to fade. "I'm sorry," she said, looking up at the others. "I don't know why I'm in such a bad mood."

"Hey, let's concentrate on trying to find Holly," said Sita. "Doing magic and helping people always makes us feel happy."

Bracken nuzzled Mia's cheek. "Can you use your mirror to try and find the dog?"

Mia nodded. She pulled the mirror out of her pocket and held it in front of her. "Holly, the Patels' dog," she told it, opening herself to the magical current. She felt it flow through her like a stream of glittering light, chasing away every

drop of irritation and tension.
At first, all she saw in the
mirror was whiteness,
but then an image of
the brown and white
spaniel appeared.
Where was she?

Mia looked more
closely, searching
for clues. Everywhere
around Holly was just
white. Suddenly, Mia realized
it was snow!

"What are you seeing?" Bracken asked her.

"Snow," she said, feeling puzzled. "But that
can't be right." She glanced out the window and
saw drizzle falling from the gray sky. There was
definitely no snow. She tried again. "Show me
where Holly, the Patels' dog, is." But the image
didn't change. "I don't know what to do. My
magic isn't showing me where she is."

"Don't worry," said Willow. "Bracken, Juniper, Sorrel, and I can go and look through the woods and countryside and see if we can find any trace of her."

Bracken jumped off Mia's knee. "We'll do it tonight."

"We'll find her," said Juniper. "And as soon as we do, we'll let you know."

Mia nodded unhappily, feeling envious of her three friends—their magic didn't seem to come and go like hers.

"You could use your magic to try and find out more about the person doing dark magic," Sita suggested.

Mia shook her head. "It never shows me anything if I ask it to show me that. Just blackness." Bracken had told her it was probably because the person was using dark magic to block herself from being discovered.

She got to her feet. "I think I might go home. I'm feeling a little strange again."

"I'll ask my dad if he'll give you a ride,"
Violet said.

Mia followed Violet down the stairs. The
happiness she had felt when she was doing
magic had vanished, and now she just felt angry
and disappointed again.

When Mia got back home, she put her school
things away, and her eyes fell on the Seeing
Stone. She picked it up, wanting to forget the
day by looking into the past. She was about to
call Bracken's name when she hesitated.

*Maybe I won't bother him—he'll be busy trying
to find Holly*, she told herself. But she knew deep
down that it was an excuse, and that really she
didn't want him there because he would try and
stop her from using the Seeing Stone.

Guilt flared inside her, but she ignored it.
"Show me Grandma Anne and Aunt Carol,"
she whispered to the stone.

A picture appeared in the surface. Grandma Anne and Aunt Carol both looked about fourteen. Aunt Carol had a crystal in her hands and was healing a scratch on Grandma Anne's leg. Grandma Anne hugged her, and then Aunt Carol showed her how she could use a different crystal to cast an illusion—making a rock beside the river appear to turn into a picnic basket. Mia was impressed—Aunt Carol could do so much with her Crystal Magic. Grandma Anne clapped and smiled.

Mia continued to stare into the stone. She lost track of time as she watched image after image of Grandma Anne and Aunt Carol. She only stopped when she felt so tired that she couldn't go on anymore.

She put down the Seeing Stone, feeling as if her energy had been sucked into it. Still, it had been worth it.

Mia placed the stone on her desk and called Bracken. He appeared instantly.

"Mia!" he said. "I've been worried about you. You didn't seem yourself earlier."

"I'm fine." Mia yawned.

Bracken sat back on his haunches. "What have you been doing?" he asked curiously.

"Just stuff." Mia shrugged.

"What stuff?" Bracken asked.

"Nothing important. Stop asking me questions!" Mia's words came out more sharply than she meant them to.

Bracken's ears flattened unhappily. Mia felt bad but couldn't bring herself to say she was sorry. She turned away and started cleaning up her desk. When she looked back, she saw Bracken had jumped onto her bed and was watching her. He looked worried.

The silence stretched between them, awkward and uncomfortable.

"I'm going downstairs to have dinner," Mia muttered, hurrying out of the room.

By the next morning, Mia was still in a bad mood, and it appeared to have spread to the rest of her family. Alex was grouchy, and Cleo was banging things around, trying to find her makeup bag. "Can't you find it for me?" she said to Mia.

"I can't find everything you lose," Mia snapped.

"Girls, please stop bickering!" Mrs. Greene said as Alex started to wail.

Mia grabbed her toast and stomped upstairs, leaving the chaos in the kitchen behind.

When she got to school, she saw Violet waiting on the playground and went over to her. Violet was holding a book on wild animals

in Africa. Mia hadn't seen it before.

"Hi," Mia muttered.

"Hi," Violet muttered back.

"What's the book for?" Mia said.

"For Lexi. Her class is doing their projects on endangered animals this week."

Mia felt a stab of jealousy. "Very friendly," she said sarcastically.

Violet frowned. "Are you jealous?" she said. "You are, aren't you? You're jealous that Lexi and I are friends now!"

"Don't be silly!" Mia retorted.

"I'm not the silly one—you are!" Violet shot back.

Just then, Lexi and Sita arrived. Lexi looked grumpy, too, but Sita was smiling as usual. "What's going on?" Sita said, looking at Mia and Violet's angry faces.

"Ask *her*," Violet and Mia muttered at the same time.

Sita looked from one friend to the other.

"Should I use my magic to help you feel better?"

"Oh, yes, your incredibly amazing magic," said Lexi. "You're such a show-off, Sita!"

"I was just trying to help," said Sita, looking upset.

"Sita isn't a show-off!" Mia said angrily.

"You always take her side!" Lexi snapped.

"No, I don't!"

"Why are you all arguing today?" Sita exclaimed.

Their squabble was interrupted by the bell

ringing. The girls picked up their bags and stomped away without saying anything more.

Mia felt like she had a black cloud hanging over her all day. Lexi and Violet seemed to feel the same, and no one suggested meeting up after school. Mia went right home and shut herself in her room. She wanted to use the Seeing Stone to see Grandma Anne again, even though she knew Bracken wouldn't like it. She thought about not calling him, but she didn't want to have to lie to him like she had the night before. Reluctantly, she called his name.

He appeared beside her. "How was school?" he asked.

Mia shrugged. "Not great." She felt suddenly upset with him. Why did he have to make her feel guilty about using the Seeing Stone? She picked it up from her desk. "I'm going to use this to see Grandma Anne."

"Mia, don't," Bracken pleaded.

"But it's better than the mirror," Mia argued. "I don't know why you're so funny about me using it." She stared into it and tried to ignore him. "Show me Grandma Anne when she was younger."

She was soon engrossed in watching Aunt Carol and Grandma Anne doing magic together. When she finally finished, she turned around to find that Bracken had curled into a small ball on her bed. Mia longed to go and cuddle him, but some part of herself stopped her.

It's not like using the Seeing Stone is really bad, she thought irritably. She got changed out of her school clothes without saying a word to Bracken, and then went downstairs. When she came back after dinner, he was gone, and she didn't call his name until bedtime. Then he just curled up quietly by her feet instead of in her arms like he usually did. She turned out the light.

8
A DIFFERENT PAST

When Mia woke up the next morning, she found that Bracken was gone. She glanced at her bedside clock and realized it was much later than usual. Where was he? He usually woke her on school mornings with licks and cuddles.

"Bracken!" she called.

He appeared in her room, beside her bed.

"Where have you been?" she asked, getting up. "You didn't wake me up, and now I'm late for school." She looked at him.

"I… I was out looking for Holly," he said.

Mia felt guilty as she realized she'd forgotten all about the lost dog. "Oh, is that why your paws are muddy?" she said, noticing Bracken's paws were flecked with soil. "Did you find her?" she asked as she started to pull on her school clothes.

"No, there's no trace of her in the woods."

"I hope she's okay," Mia said anxiously. "Maybe I should use the Seeing Stone to try and see her again."

"No, don't!" Bracken said quickly.

Mia frowned. The Seeing Stone wasn't on her desk where she'd left it. She crouched down to check the floor, but just then, her dad knocked on the door and opened it. Bracken vanished just in time.

"Come on, Mia. What are you doing? You're going to be late for school. You need to have some breakfast."

Mia had no choice but to follow her dad

downstairs. *I'll find the Seeing Stone later*, she thought uneasily.

However, when Mia got back from school, she couldn't find the Seeing Stone anywhere. She called Bracken.

"It couldn't have just vanished into thin air," she said. "Have you seen it?"

Bracken scratched his ear with his back paw as he watched her search. "No."

Mia felt a flash of anger. "What am I going to do? I need it!"

"You don't need it," said Bracken, trotting over to her. "You can use Star Magic."

It doesn't work as well, Mia thought, but she didn't say anything to Bracken.

"You can," Bracken insisted, jumping up onto her lap. "Why don't you try now?"

"There's no point," Mia muttered, rubbing his fur. "It won't work."

Bracken cocked his head to one side. "Is that what you think?"

She nodded.

"But Mia, you can't think like that." He looked at her earnestly. "Remember when you first started learning to do magic, and I said it would only happen if you believed it would? If you don't believe the magic will work, it won't."

Mia frowned. She'd forgotten that.

"Seeing magic *is* hard to control," Bracken went on. "But it won't help if you think it's not going to work."

"Maybe I'll try again," Mia said, feeling her bad mood start to fade. She stared into the mirror on the dressing table, petting Bracken as she did. "Show me, Holly," she said, hoping she would get more of an idea of where Holly was this time.

She leaned forward eagerly as an image gradually formed in the mirror, but it just showed Holly surrounded by a lot of snow again. Mia couldn't understand what was going on.

She frowned. Was her magic working? She decided to try something else. "Show me Grandma Anne when she and Aunt Carol were my age," she said.

The surface of the mirror swirled like liquid silver, and Mia's heart gave a leap as an image of Grandma Anne and Aunt Carol appeared. They were both wearing old-fashioned school uniforms. Aunt Carol was glaring at Grandma Anne and speaking angrily. She could hear Aunt Carol saying, "It's not fair! Everyone likes you, Anne. Everyone wants to be your friend. No one wants to be mine!"

"That's not true, Carol," said Grandma Anne. "I'm your friend."

"Yes, but you like everyone!" said Aunt Carol, and then she turned and ran away.

Mia sat back in surprise. She'd never seen Aunt Carol and Grandma Anne arguing before.

"Show me Grandma Anne and Aunt Carol when they start doing magic," she said curiously.

The image changed, and she saw Grandma Anne with her hand on her wolf's back, staring at Aunt Carol, who seemed to be hovering behind a blackberry bush as if she'd been hiding. "You can't tell anyone, Carol," Grandma Anne pleaded. "No one is supposed to know about Star Magic. Promise you won't say a word!"

Mia blinked. Weird. She'd seen this moment in the past before, but it hadn't been like this. When she'd seen it in the Seeing Stone, Grandma Anne had been excitedly telling Aunt Carol that she had a secret to share with her. Now Grandma Anne seemed to be begging Aunt Carol not to say anything—almost as if Grandma Anne hadn't wanted Aunt Carol to know....

"This is odd," Mia whispered to Bracken. "I'm seeing a different past than the one I've seen in the Seeing Stone."

"A different past?" He tilted his head. "But there can't be two pasts."

"I don't know which one is real," said Mia. "Show me more," she said to the mirror.

The image changed, and Mia saw Aunt Carol in the clearing with Grandma Anne. They were older now—teenagers. "I can do magic, too," Aunt Carol was saying to Grandma Anne, showing her a crystal. "It's not just you now. I'm special, too!"

"Yes," Grandma Anne said slowly, "but you must be careful. Magic should only be used for good. Please only do good things with it."

Aunt Carol smiled slyly as she turned the crystal over in her hand. "We'll see."

Mia sat back and let the images fade. "In the

Seeing Stone, I see Grandma Anne and Aunt Carol as really good friends, but when I look with Star Magic, it's not quite like that. Why?"

"I don't know," Bracken said anxiously. "But I think you should believe what the Star Magic is showing you."

Mia rubbed him. "I wish I knew where the Seeing Stone was."

Bracken nuzzled her. "Maybe you should stop doing magic for tonight. We can talk to the other animals tomorrow and see if they have any idea about why the things you're seeing are different."

When Mia went to sleep, she had the first vivid dream she'd had in a long time. Bracken had told her that her dreams might show real things now that her magic was growing stronger. For a while, they had—she'd seen the Fear Shades before they started affecting people—but for the last couple of weeks, her dreams hadn't shown her anything at all. Tonight was different, though.

In her dream, Grandma Anne and Aunt

Carol were in the clearing. They looked about sixteen years old.

Aunt Carol's eyes were shining. "Crystals have energy inside them," she said to Grandma Anne. "All you have to do is figure out how to channel it, and then you can use it for anything you want. You can make an object look like something else! They can heal, hurt, upset—"

"But magic should only be used for good," Grandma Anne interrupted. "You know that."

"But why?" said Aunt Carol. "We could get revenge on people who have made us miserable."

"No!" Grandma Anne exclaimed. "You can't do that."

Aunt Carol smiled. "When I possess the Dark Stone, no one will be able to stop me. Not even you." She laughed.

Mia sat up in bed, her heart pounding. Had her dream been real? It couldn't be. Aunt Carol wouldn't use magic to do bad things. Bracken was still snoozing beside her. Dawn was just breaking, the dark of night turning to a cold gray.

Mia went to her desk to look for the Seeing Stone. How could it have just vanished? Then she looked into the mirror and had an idea. Of course! She could use Star Magic to see where it was.

She opened herself to the magic current. "Show me where the Seeing Stone is."

A picture of her backyard appeared in the mirror.

But how can it be in the yard? she wondered.

"Show me how the Seeing Stone got there," she said curiously.

The image reformed. Ice seemed to run down her spine as she saw a fox trotting toward the flower bed just as dawn was breaking. It was Bracken, and he had the Seeing Stone in his mouth. She watched as he dropped it onto the soil, dug a hole, and nudged it inside.

Bracken had taken the Seeing Stone. He had

lied to her! Unless … unless what she was seeing was false.

"Bracken!" she said, swinging around.

He woke instantly. "What is it?" he said, jumping to his feet.

"Did you take the Seeing Stone?" she demanded. "Did you bury it in the yard?" She was sure he was going to shake his head and tell her that what she had seen wasn't true.

But he looked down at the bed. "Yes," he admitted. "I'm sorry. But I didn't like you using it. There's something strange about it, Mia. I think it's showing you a false past, and I think it's doing something to your Star Magic…."

"How dare you!" Mia hissed. She grabbed her robe and slippers. "I'm going to get it back!"

"Mia!" Bracken protested. "Don't go!"

"You're the one who should go," Mia said. "I don't want you here!"

Bracken whimpered. "You don't mean that."

"I do! Go!"

Mia ran out of her room, down the stairs, and through the back door. A light frost covered the grass, and the air stung her cheeks. She ran to the flower bed that she had seen in the mirror and spotted a patch of soil that looked like it had been recently disturbed. Crouching down, she used her hands to dig into the freezing soil. She caught a glimmer of pink and pushed the soil to one side. It was the Seeing Stone! She took it out with a sigh of relief.

When she came back into the house, her dad was in the kitchen getting Alex a bottle of milk.

"Mia!" he exclaimed. "What on earth are you doing out in the yard at this hour?"

"I'd left something out there," Mia lied.

"Well, you don't go out at six in the morning! And look at the mess you're making on the carpet."

"I'm sorry," Mia said. "I'll clean it up."

"Just take off your slippers and get back upstairs," her dad snapped. "I don't want this to happen again."

Mia kicked off her slippers and ran upstairs. When she got back to her room, it was empty. Bracken was gone.

9
MAKING PLANS

Mia shut the door and walked slowly over to her bed. Her eyes filled with hot, stinging tears. Everything was wrong. Everyone was angry and arguing, and Bracken…. She thought back to how she had told him to go, and a sudden fear gripped her. He wouldn't have gone back to the Star World, would he? He *was* still her Star Animal, right?

She sat on the bed and put her face in her hands.

"Bracken," she whispered.

She held her breath. Nothing happened. Her heart felt like it was going to break into pieces.

"Bracken!" she whispered frantically.

She almost fainted with relief when a shimmer of starlight slowly appeared, a curling plume of light getting stronger until it turned into the shape of a fox.

Bracken stood across the room from her, his ears lowered sadly and his tail between his legs.

"Bracken!" Mia gasped, holding out her arms.

He crept slowly over to her, wagging the tip of his bushy tail, and she gathered him into her arms.

"I thought you'd gone back to the Star
World," she said, a tear spilling down her cheek.
"I thought I wasn't ever going to see you
again."

He licked the tear away. "You're my Star
Friend, Mia. That means I'll be with you for
your whole life. If you call me, I'll always
come."

"I'm sorry." Mia hugged him as tightly as
she could. As he snuggled in her arms, she felt
the anger that had been filling her mind drain
away.

"I'm sorry I took the Seeing Stone, and I'm
sorry I lied to you," he told her. "I just don't
like that stone. I think there's something strange
about it."

"I won't use it again," said Mia. "And I…
I'm sorry I snapped at you the other day.
I've just felt so mixed up and confused. It's
like there's a cloud in my head making me
feel angry all the time at the moment." She

frowned. "Though it's not there now."

Bracken looked thoughtful. "I wonder if…."
He broke off. "Stay there. Let's try something."
He wriggled out of her arms and trotted across
her bedroom. "How do you feel now?"

Irritation started to flicker through Mia.
"Worse again."

Bracken bounded back and jumped into her
arms. "And now?" he said, nuzzling her neck.

The feelings faded.

"Better," said Mia. She frowned at him. "So,
when I'm hugging you, I feel normal. Why?"

"The bad feelings must be caused by some
sort of dark magic," Bracken said, his indigo
eyes serious. "That's why they go away when
you're hugging me."

"Do you think there's a Shade in the house?"
said Mia, looking around her room. "Everyone
in my family has been in a bad mood. Lexi
and Violet, too. Do you think there are a lot
of Shades?"

"Maybe," said Bracken. "I think we need to speak to the others."

"I'll ask them to meet me before school," said Mia. She jumped up to get her phone. As soon as she was no longer holding Bracken, she could feel the bad mood starting to take over again, but she tried to fight the feelings away. *I'm not upset*, she told herself firmly. *I'm not angry.* She sent a group message to the others.

Must talk to you at school. It's important. Get there early. Mxx

A few seconds later, her phone pinged. It was a message from Lexi.

I can't. Gotta go to dentist Lx

Mia wanted to talk to everyone together. She texted back:

Okay. Let's meet at recess and talk then.

Her phone pinged once more. It was Violet.

What's going on? Vx

Tell u later. But for now cuddle ur animals a lot.

WHAT?!!

Sita joined in.

I don't understand. Sxxx

Talk at schl. Try not to get angry. Mxx

And then, ignoring the flurry of question marks and confused emojis that started showing up on her phone from her friends, she gathered Bracken into her arms and hugged him tightly.

✦ ✦ ✦

"So, you're saying you think Shades have been making us argue?" Violet said in a low voice as they sat on the wall at recess. They were all wrapped up in coats and scarves and hats against the cold.

Mia nodded. "We don't normally feel like this, do we? We don't usually fall out like we did yesterday. My family has been in bad moods, too."

"And mine," said Lexi. "Mom's been shouting all the time."

Violet nodded. "Mine, too."

"Mine haven't," said Sita, looking puzzled. "And I haven't felt angry. I have felt unhappy, but that's just because everyone's been arguing."

Mia looked at Lexi and Violet. "But you've felt like me? Like there's something making you feel angry with everyone."

They both nodded.

"I shouted at Sorrel yesterday," Violet admitted.

"And I got upset with Juniper," said Lexi.

"I told Bracken to go away," said Mia.

"It's got to be because of Shades," Sita said. "Maybe they're just affecting me differently."

Lexi rolled her eyes. "Oh, because you're so special!" Her hand flew to her mouth. "I'm sorry!" she gasped. "I didn't mean that, Sita! I don't know why I said it. I feel all twisted up inside with horrible feelings. Mia's right. It's *got* to be because of Shades."

"But where are they? What are they trapped in this time?" said Violet. "Why haven't Sorrel or Willow smelled them? They're both really good at sniffing out Shades."

"I don't know," said Mia. "Should we meet up after school and try to figure it out?"

"I can't. I'm going over to my grandma's," Sita said.

"And I have piano until six," said Lexi.

"I could ask Sorrel to check my house really well," said Violet. "And then later I'll shadow-travel to Mia and Lexi's and bring us all to yours, Sita. Can you make sure no one is in your clubhouse? We could meet there."

Sita nodded.

"Okay, Mia and Lexi, be ready in your bedrooms at six-thirty. Agreed?" said Violet.

Mia felt a rush of irritation that Violet was taking charge, but she pushed it firmly away. "Okay. And in the meantime, let's try really hard not to argue."

They all nodded. "Agreed."

Mia found it hard to concentrate at school that day. She realized she hadn't told the others about the different pasts she had seen when she was using the Seeing Stone and the Star Magic, but right now, it felt more important to stop the Shades that were making them argue.

When she got home, she shut herself away in her bedroom with Bracken and lay on her bed cuddling him. A little later, she got a text from Sita.

How r u? Sxxx

OK. Did u see ur grandma?

Yes. She wasn't in a v good mood, either.
Maybe there are Shades EVERYWHERE!

Mia bit her lip.

Want to talk? Mxx

After a few seconds, her phone started to ring with a video call from Sita.

Mia answered it, and Sita's face appeared on her screen. She looked upset.

"What if I'm right? What if there are Shades everywhere, and they're affecting everyone?" she said.

"We'll get rid of them," Mia told her. "We're Star Friends. You'll be able to command them like you did with the stretchy men."

"If it works," said Sita. "I haven't tried it since…. Mia, what if it doesn't?"

"It will," Mia told her. "But first we have to *find* the Shades. Did Willow notice any trace at your house?"

"Nothing," said Sita. "But maybe Sorrel has found something at Violet's."

"I hope so," said Mia.

When it got close to six-thirty, they hung up, and Mia waited for Violet to appear. Even though she was expecting it, she still jumped when Violet and Lexi stepped out of the shadows beside her closet.

"Let's get to Sita's," Violet said, holding out her hand.

Mia stepped into the shadows with Violet and Lexi and felt the strange sensation of the world spinning away around her. Then her feet touched solid ground, and she realized that she was standing in Sita's clubhouse. It was a garden shed that Sita and her sisters had put a rug and some beanbags in.

Sita had turned on a small table light, casting shadows against the shed walls. "We can't be long," she said anxiously. "Our parents might start wondering where we are."

"Did Sorrel find anything?" Mia asked Violet.

"No, nothing," Violet said. "She went through my whole house, and she didn't smell a Shade anywhere."

"But there have to be Shades there!" said Mia.

"Maybe magic can disguise the smell," said Lexi.

"I asked Sorrel that," Violet said. "She said nothing can hide the smell of Shades."

"It doesn't make sense," said Mia. "The bad

moods have to be caused by Shades, because otherwise, they wouldn't fade like they do when we're cuddling our animals."

Sita glanced out the window anxiously. "I'm going to have to go inside in a minute."

"Let's meet up tomorrow morning," said Mia. "Is everyone free?"

They found out they were all free except for Lexi, who had gymnastics. "I can meet you right after," she said.

"Why don't we meet at my house at twelve," said Violet. "We can go to the clearing in the woods. Maybe we'll think better when we're there because Sorrel says the current of magic is so strong."

"Then it's the Christmas fair in the afternoon," said Mia.

Sita shivered. "It's creepy to think that the person doing dark magic might actually be there. We might speak to her without realizing it."

"We've got to make a list of everyone we see

there who matches the description," said Lexi. "The sooner we find out who it is, the better!"

Violet shadow-traveled them all home. After Mia had whispered good-bye and her friends had disappeared, she sat down at her desk feeling very confused. If there were Shades affecting them all, why couldn't Sorrel and Willow find any trace of them?

I don't get it, she thought, resting her chin on her hands and staring into the mirror. *I don't understand.*

10
A Troubling Visit

Mia's dreams that night showed her a gloomy underground room with stone walls. She was trapped, unable to move and overwhelmed by the feeling that she had lost something precious. A woman in a hooded cloak stalked up to her with a dark crystal in her hand. Mia could not see her face.

"When I touch you with this, you will lose everything," hissed the woman. She lifted it toward Mia.

"No!" Mia screamed.

She woke with a start to find Bracken licking her face. "You were having a bad dream, Mia. You were calling out in your sleep."

Mia pulled Bracken into a hug, burying her face in his soft fur, and told him what she'd seen.

"What did the woman look like?" Bracken asked. "Was it anyone you recognized?"

"I couldn't see her face." Mia shuddered as she remembered the fear she'd felt.

Bracken cuddled her closer. "We have to figure out what's going on. Maybe when you go to the fair this afternoon, you'll find some clues about who the lady is who's doing all this."

"I hope so," said Mia.

She lay in bed and petted Bracken until it was time to get up.

She was just getting dressed when her phone pinged.

It was a message from Sita.

What r u doing this morning? Sxx

Nothing. What about u?

Nothing much either. I didn't sleep v well. Think I might go and see Aunt Carol and have a talk with her about my power.

Good plan. Come here afterward if u want.

OK! Sxx

Mia put her phone into her pocket and kissed Bracken. "I'm going to get some breakfast. Sita's coming over later. Maybe we can do some magic with her and Willow."

She went downstairs. Her mom was banging breakfast bowls on the table. "Are you okay?" Mia asked tentatively.

"No, not really. I have so much to do," her mom said. "I need to help set up for the fair this morning, but I also have to show someone Grandma Anne's house. And I said I would stop by and help Aunt Carol take some boxes of decorations to the hall."

"I can do that," said Mia. Then she could meet Sita there, and they could both talk to Aunt Carol. Maybe Aunt Carol would be able to help her figure out why she was seeing two different versions of the past.

"Well, I was going to drive the boxes of decorations to the hall," her mom said, "but I'm sure they're light enough for you to carry. That would really help." She smiled. "Thanks, sweetie."

"No problem. I'll go after breakfast," Mia said, putting some bread in the toaster.

✸ ✸ ✸

After breakfast, Mia ran upstairs to tell Bracken what she was doing. "I'll be back as soon as I can," she said.

"All right." He licked her nose as she hugged him. "I'll see you later."

He jumped onto the bed and curled up into a ball, his nose tucked into his bushy tail.

Mia smiled. "I love you," she whispered,
giving him a kiss. She picked up the Seeing
Stone so she could ask Aunt Carol about it and
texted Sita as she headed out.

Are u at AC's yet? I'll c u there. Mxx

Mia rode her bike quickly to keep warm.
By the time she reached Aunt Carol's house,
her cheeks were pink, and she was slightly
breathless.

"Good morning," said Aunt Carol, opening
the door when she knocked. "What are you
doing here, Mia?"

"I've come to help you take the decorations
to the hall—Mom's really busy with other
things," said Mia.

"That's very kind of you," said Aunt Carol.

"Is Sita here?" Mia asked.

Aunt Carol looked surprised. "Sita? No.
Why? Was she planning on visiting me?"

Mia nodded. "She's going to drop by this morning. She wants to talk to you about magic," she said as Aunt Carol ushered her inside.

"Well, why don't I get you a hot chocolate while we're waiting for her?" said Aunt Carol. "You go on into the living room, and I'll put the kettle on."

As Aunt Carol hurried to the kitchen, Mia took off her coat and hung it in the hall, making a mental note that Aunt Carol seemed as cheerful as usual. *No Shades affecting her,* she thought as she went into the living room.

The boxes of knitted decorations sat on the coffee table. Mia picked one up, and its black crystal eyes sparkled in the light. Although the decoration looked cute, the crystal reminded Mia of the dark crystal she had seen in her dream. She shivered and put down the decoration.

The large snow globe she had seen the last time she was here was standing on the mantel. She went over to it and saw that it now had a little model of a brown and white dog inside, curled up, fast asleep. How had Aunt Carol put that in there?

Magic? wondered Mia.

Then the dog yawned and sat up.

Mia squeaked in shock. The dog was moving! It shook itself and sniffed around in the snow. Mia stared. What amazing magic was making the model dog seem alive?

She skirted around it to examine the globe from a different angle. The little brown and white dog looked strangely familiar, Mia decided. It looked just like Holly, the Patels' missing dog! As she stepped to the side to get a closer look, she stepped on something soft and glanced down to see a blue and white scarf with a polka-dot pattern. Mia froze. It was Sita's favorite scarf.

But Aunt Carol had just told her that Sita hadn't stopped by.

Her fingers tightened on the soft fabric, unease quickening through her as she looked from the scarf to the snow globe. What was going on?

Then she heard a faint banging sound coming from the hallway. Picking up the snow globe, she hurried to the living room doorway.

Thump, thump, thump.

The noise was coming from the door under the stairs. Mia knew that it led to Aunt Carol's cellar. Her heart skipped a beat as she heard a faint voice. "Let me out! Please, let me out!"

"Sita?" Mia gasped in shock.

"Mia! Get me out of here!" Sita exclaimed.

Mia put the snow globe on the floor and started to pull the stiff metal bolts on the door.

"What are you doing in there?" she whispered as she tried to wriggle the top bolt back.

"Aunt Carol locked me in," said Sita, her voice faint through the door. "Mia, we've got to get out of here. She's not good like we thought."

Mia felt like all the breath had left her body. "What?"

"She's trapped Holly in the snow globe! She's evil!" Sita said.

There was a laugh behind her. Mia spun around and saw Aunt Carol standing in the kitchen doorway, watching her with an amused look in her eyes.

11
TRAPPED!

Aunt Carol's smile widened as Mia stared at her.

"Mia!" Sita banged on the door, breaking Mia out of her shock. "What's happening?"

Throwing herself at the door again, Mia scrambled to pull back the bolts.

"Bracken!" she gasped. "Please come! I need you!"

He appeared in a shimmer of starlight just as Aunt Carol pulled a dark crystal from her pocket and held it out toward the door, muttering a harsh-sounding word that Mia had never heard before. The metal bolts instantly turned red-hot.

Mia yelped and pulled her hands away, her fingers stinging.

"Let Sita out!" shouted Mia as Bracken bounded at Aunt Carol, his teeth bared, and stopped in front of her, growling angrily. "Why have you locked her up?"

Aunt Carol grabbed the snow globe from the floor where Mia had left it.

"Because I am going to stop you Star Friends from getting in my way," Aunt Carol said. She held the snow globe in one hand and a large, glittering dark crystal in the other.

A shiver ran down Mia's spine as she recognized the crystal from her dream.

Bracken sprang forward, and for a moment, Mia thought he was going to be able to snatch it—but then Aunt Carol swung the snow globe at him. The instant it touched his fur, he vanished.

Mia stared at the empty space where he had been. "Bracken!" Her voice rose. "What have you done with him?"

Aunt Carol held up the snow globe with a triumphant smile. Inside the globe, next to the little dog, there was now a small russet fox. "He's in here. And unless you do what I say, you won't ever see him again."

"Bracken!" Mia whispered, horrified.

Bracken started to bark furiously—Mia could see his mouth opening and closing, but she couldn't hear him. Aunt Carol touched the Dark Stone to the bolts of the cellar door, and they slid back on their own, opening the door.

There was a flash of brown, and Willow came charging out, heading straight for Aunt Carol.

"Willow! Be careful!" cried Sita.

Moving more swiftly than Mia would have thought possible, Aunt Carol swept the globe toward Willow, and as it touched her back, the deer vanished.

"Two Star Animals are mine, just two to go!" crowed Aunt Carol, holding up the globe. Inside, Willow was standing next to Bracken, shaking her head and looking very surprised.

"Into the cellar with your friend!" Aunt Carol commanded, looking at Mia.

"No." Mia shook her head. "I'm not going in there."

"If you don't, I will smash the globe. And what will happen to your precious animals then?" Aunt Carol's eyes met Mia's. "They'll be gone forever!" She held the globe high above the floor.

"Stop it!" Sita cried, but Aunt Carol ignored her.

Mia hesitated. What should she do? Aunt Carol's hand started to swing the globe downward.

"No! Wait!" Mia gasped. "I'll go in the cellar."

She joined Sita, and with a harsh laugh, Aunt Carol swung the door shut, plunging them into darkness. As they heard the bolts being pushed across, Sita grabbed Mia's hands. "What are we going to do?"

"I... I don't know." Mia was struggling to take everything in. Bracken was gone, and so was Willow.... She and Sita were trapped.... And Aunt Carol had been the person using dark magic!

Mia peered through the gloom. They were at the top of a staircase that led down into the cellar. "Isn't there a light in here?"

"I haven't been able to find one," said Sita.

Mia drew on her magic. It tingled through her and her eyesight sharpened, letting her see through the gloom.

"There!" she said, spotting an old-fashioned metal light switch high up on the wall.

Standing on tiptoe, she pressed it, and a bulb in the ceiling lit up. It cast a weak light. At the bottom of the wooden stairs, the shadows in the cellar seemed to make everything look menacing. Still, it was better to have some light than none at all.

"What's she going to do to Bracken and Willow?" said Sita.

"I don't know." Mia felt panic rising inside her, but she forced it down. Panicking wouldn't help them—or their animals. "We have to get them out of that globe." She frowned. "How did you end up trapped here?"

Sita shivered. "When I came over to talk to Aunt Carol, she said she would make me some hot chocolate. As I was drinking it, I noticed the snow globe. Did you see it? Holly's inside!"

"I know! I saw!" Mia said. "Then I noticed your scarf on the floor."

"I must have dropped it when I saw Holly," Sita went on. "I think Aunt Carol put something in the hot chocolate. All I can remember is jumping up to leave but then feeling really dizzy. I must have passed out because when I woke up, I was in here. I called Willow and started banging on the door, and then I heard you on the other side. Now you're in here, too!" Her eyes filled with tears.

Mia hugged her. "Aunt Carol can't keep us in here forever," she said. "When she comes back, you'll have to use your commanding magic and make her let us out."

"It doesn't work," said Sita. "I tried when she was about to smash the globe, but it didn't make any difference."

Mia's heart sank. "You were trying to use your magic then?"

Sita nodded. "I can't do it. I told you. It was just a fluke with the stretchy men." She wiped away her tears with the back of her hand. "I'm not that powerful."

"Don't worry," Mia said. "I'll come up with another way to get us out." She thought back over the last few months. So, Aunt Carol had been the person doing evil all along. She must have attached the stretchy men to the boxes of sparklers herself. Mia remembered what the sales assistant at the garden center had said to

Violet and Lexi—an older lady with gray hair
and blue eyes had bought the Wish Gnome.
That must have been Aunt Carol, too. And then
there was the very first Shade they had faced—
the one who had been trapped inside the old
compact mirror talking to Cleo. A picture
flashed into Mia's mind of Aunt Carol helping
her mom clean out Grandma Anne's house....

"Look what I just found in a drawer," she'd
said, turning around to Mia with the compact
mirror in her hand.

*Maybe she took it with her and gave it to me on
purpose,* Mia realized. *She wanted me to be affected
by the Shade—only I gave the compact to Cleo.
Aunt Carol found the compact just after I had told
her I had seen a fox with indigo eyes. She must have
realized I was going to be a Star Friend.*

She felt sick. She had trusted Aunt Carol.
She had told her about Bracken and let her
see the Star Animals. She had asked her for
advice and taken it. When she had tried to do

what Aunt Carol said, her magic had stopped working, too. Why hadn't she realized?

Because I thought Aunt Carol was Grandma Anne's friend!

Mia remembered the two different pasts she had seen—one using Star Magic and one using the Seeing Stone. She pulled the pink Seeing Stone out of her pocket and it glittered in the dim light. No wonder Bracken hadn't liked it. It had been showing her lies about the past. She looked at the golden glow coming from it and groaned inwardly. She should have realized. Whenever something was under an illusion spell, she saw a glow around it. "I don't believe you look like you do," she whispered.

The glow faded, and the stone turned an ugly gray with a red eye-shape in the center.

"What's that stone?" Sita said curiously.

"Aunt Carol gave it to me," Mia said. "She told me it would help me see into the past, but it hasn't been showing me the real past.

It's been showing me a past she wanted me to see. Aunt Carol wanted me to think that she and Grandma Anne were really good friends. I guess she did it so that I would trust her."

"But they *were* friends, weren't they?" Sita said, looking confused. "Didn't your grandma visit her a lot?"

Mia nodded. She didn't understand that part. Why *had* Grandma Anne visited Aunt Carol so often if Aunt Carol was evil?

She threw the Seeing Stone away from her, down the stairs into the shadows, and heard it clatter onto the stone floor.

Just then, there was the sound of the bolts pulling back. The girls jumped to their feet as the door opened and Aunt Carol stood there, smiling at them, the snow globe in one hand, the Dark Stone in the other.

12

A Desperate Situation

"Let us go!" Sita said. She took a breath, and Mia could tell she was trying to use her commanding magic. Her voice shook. "You must let us out of here."

Aunt Carol laughed. "Oh, no. You're not going anywhere."

She held up the glittering Dark Stone, and Mia cried out as a stream of energy seemed to thump into her stomach. Arms windmilling, she fell backward, and she and Sita tumbled down the stairs in a tangle of arms and legs.

They landed in a heap in the cellar. Aunt
Carol chuckled and followed them down to
the bottom.

For a moment, Mia was winded and
struggled to breathe. She rolled onto her knees,
drawing in gasps of air, and saw that Sita was
doing the same.

Mia was aware of Aunt Carol moving swiftly
around them. But it was only as she got her
breath back that she realized Aunt Carol had
drawn a circle around them using the stone,
leaving a glowing red line on the floor. Aunt

Carol straightened up and muttered a word. Instantly, an assortment of candles standing on ledges around the stone cellar lit up. They cast a flickering glow, letting Mia see that they were in a large underground room with a table at one end covered in rocks and crystals.

"What are you doing?" Mia demanded, standing up and helping Sita to her feet.

"I'm using the Dark Stone to make sure you can't escape," said Aunt Carol coldly. "I will keep you here until your friends arrive. When I have their Star Animals, too, I will use the Dark Stone to take away all your memories of magic. I will make you forget you ever knew about Star Animals and the Star World. When you stop believing in magic, you will no longer stand in my way."

"We'll never stop believing in magic!" exclaimed Mia.

Aunt Carol's eyes glittered. "You will not be able to resist the Dark Stone. It is one of

the most powerful crystals in the world. You're going to have to say good-bye to your animals."

She held out the snow globe. Bracken put up his paws on the glass, looking desperately at Mia. She lunged forward, but flames leaped up from the glowing line on the floor, licking at her outstretched arms. Mia sprang back.

"Why are you doing this?" shouted Sita.

"Why?" Aunt Carol raised her eyebrows. "So that I can be the most powerful. More powerful than any Star Friend will ever be."

"I thought you and Grandma Anne were friends!" Mia said furiously, her eyes stinging with tears. "I thought you did good magic!"

Aunt Carol snorted. "That's what she would have liked. But then I found the Dark Stone, and I knew that when I learned to use it, I would be able to do anything I wanted." Her voice grew bitter. "But before I could learn to use its powers properly, Anne managed to take it from me and use her commanding magic to stop me from taking it back. Every time she visited me, she reinforced the command—and without the Dark Stone, I was powerless to fight back."

"So that's why she visited you so often," Mia said slowly.

Aunt Carol gave a nod. "People thought we were friends, but really, she was just trying to get me to lead a normal life. A dull life without magic and power while she—" her eyes filled with jealousy—"could continue doing her magic. She had her Star Animal. I had nothing!"

"She stopped you because you were going

to use magic for bad things," said Mia. "You wanted to hurt people—just like you're doing now." She looked at the stone. "But how did you get the stone back?"

"Oh, I was so helpful when your grandma died, wasn't I?" Aunt Carol said with a sly smile. "I offered to clean through all her things, and I found it. It was as if it was waiting for me." Her fingers clenched around it. "Now it's mine, and I am going to use it to hurt all the people Anne wanted to protect."

"What do you mean?" said Sita.

"Those knitted decorations upstairs are so sweet, aren't they?" said Aunt Carol. "I'm sure they'll sell out at the fair today. Once they're in houses all around town, they'll start to affect people, little by little."

"The decorations?" Mia said. "But they don't have Shades in them. Sorrel checked."

"Oh, my dear, you have so much to learn. It's not only Shades that can cause trouble," said

Aunt Carol. "Herbs, potions, crystals, spells—they can all be used to release negative energy that will hurt and harm. Like that Seeing Stone I glamoured and gave to you. It showed you a false past, and it has also been sending out negative energy to block your magic and stop it from working."

Mia stared at her. Now that she thought about it, she realized it was true. Aunt Carol laughed at her stunned expression.

"You really have been so easy to deceive. Those crystals I carefully sewed into the eyes of the decorations will send out their negative energy. People will start to be affected, and unhappiness will come. But no one will ever suspect the innocent little decorations. No one will be having a good Christmas in Westport this year." She smiled in delight.

"We'll stop you!" Mia exclaimed.

"How?" said Aunt Carol, raising her eyebrows. "You're trapped here. Soon your

friends will be here with you, too, and then
I will take all your memories of magic away.
If you don't believe, you can't make magic
happen."

"But how will you get the others to come
here?" said Sita.

"By using a little illusion combined with
modern technology." Her voice hardened.
"Star Friends always think they're so special.
But Crystal Magic is better. You each only
have a few powers—I can do many things!"
She walked to the table and put down the
snow globe. Then she held up the Dark Stone
and whispered Mia's name. The air seemed to
shiver, and Aunt Carol changed to look just like
Mia. "What do you think?"

"You won't fool Lexi and Violet!" Mia
declared.

"You don't sound like Mia," said Sita.

Aunt Carol held the stone to her throat and
muttered another word.

"I'll be back very soon," she said in Mia's voice and then, picking up the snow globe, she laughed and headed up the stairs.

13
WHAT NOW?

"What are we going to do?" Mia said desperately as they heard the cellar door shut.

"I don't know," said Sita. "But let me heal the burn on your arm first." She took Mia's arm, and Mia felt as if a cooling breeze was sweeping over her skin, taking away the heat and pain. She watched the blisters disappear and the pinkness fade.

"Thank you," she said gratefully.

"At least I can still do that type of magic," said Sita with relief.

"I bet you can do your commanding magic, too," said Mia. Sita shook her head, but Aunt Carol's words were echoing in Mia's head: *If you don't believe, you can't make magic happen.* It reminded her of what Bracken had said. "When you try to do it, do you believe it will work?"

Sita hesitated. "Um … not really, I guess. It's not how I feel with healing magic. I know that will work."

"You need to believe your commanding magic will work, too," said Mia. "When the Seeing Stone was affecting me, I stopped thinking that my Star Magic would show me the past. Even when I wasn't near the Seeing Stone, it didn't work. But once I believed it would, it did." Mia looked around for some way to escape. Right now, persuading Sita her magic would work wasn't the priority. "We need to get to Violet and Lexi somehow and warn them."

Sita gasped. "My phone! We could use it to text them!" She pulled it out of her pocket and tried to turn it on, but then her face fell. "It's not working. The battery must be dead."

"Or the magic in here is stopping it somehow," said Mia.

"Where's yours?" said Sita.

"In my coat in the hallway," said Mia. "We've got to think of a plan. I wonder how much time we have. If Aunt Carol is going to persuade Lexi and Violet to come here, it'll take her a little while. I can use my magic to see where they are." She took the mirror out of her pocket and tried to relax. "Lexi," she whispered.

An image of Lexi appeared. She was just going into Violet's house. "They're at Violet's," Mia said to Sita. She watched Violet and Lexi run upstairs and go into Violet's bedroom.

"The others will be here soon," she heard Violet say. "I wonder if we'll find out anything about the person doing dark magic at the fair this afternoon."

Suddenly, Violet's phone rang, and she picked it up from her desk. "Mia's calling me."

Mia frowned. Aunt Carol must have taken her phone! "Don't answer it!" she pleaded, even though she knew they couldn't hear her.

"What's happening?" demanded Sita.

Mia shook her head—she needed to see what was happening. Violet was answering the call, and a picture of Mia popped up on her screen. "Hi, it's me."

It was really odd for Mia to hear her own voice.

"Where are you?" Violet asked, holding up the phone so Lexi could join in with the call.

"At Aunt Carol's. I need you both to come here quickly."

"Why?" said Lexi.

"I've found something very important in the cellar. Come now."

"Okay," said Violet. "But what is it?"

"I'll tell you when you get here."

The phone went blank.

Mia's face paled, and she told Sita what had just happened.

"We've got to think of some way to stop them," said Sita.

There was a crash and a clatter beside the table, and Violet and Lexi appeared in the shadows with Sorrel and Juniper.

Mia's heart plummeted. It was too late.

Sorrel took one sniff of the air, and her tail fluffed up in alarm.

"What's going on?" Violet demanded, hurrying toward Mia and Sita.

Sorrel yowled and leaped in front of Violet, knocking her over. Violet sprawled on the stone floor. "What did you do that for?" she gasped.

"Dark magic!" Sorrel hissed, her indigo eyes flashing as she looked at the circle on the floor. She spun around, taking in everything in the room. "This place reeks of it!"

"Sorrel's right," Mia said. "Whatever you do, don't try and cross over the circle drawn on the floor. Flames jump up at you. You'll get burned."

Violet scrambled to her feet, and Lexi joined her. Juniper was next to her, looking around anxiously.

"What's going on?" Lexi demanded again.

Mia and Sita told them about Aunt Carol. They both looked stunned.

"I knew it!" spat Sorrel. "When we were in her yard last time, I smelled Shades."

"We thought it was because of Mrs. Crooks," said Mia, "but it must have been because of Aunt Carol. She has a stone that's really powerful. Grandma Anne took it from her a long time ago and then visited her every day to keep commanding her not to use dark magic. But when Grandma Anne died, Aunt Carol got the stone back."

"I just can't believe it," said Lexi, shaking her head.

"It's true," said Sita. She told them about the illusion Aunt Carol had cast to make herself look and sound like Mia. "She's probably waiting for you at the front door right now."

"Why did you come to the cellar?" said Mia.

"Well, you said you'd found something important here—I wanted to find out what it was," said Violet.

"Violet's so brave," said Sorrel, purring approvingly and weaving between Violet's legs.

"I tried to stop her," said Lexi. "Though I'm

kind of glad she didn't listen to me now. At least we didn't walk right into a trap."

"Where are Bracken and Willow?" said Juniper looking around.

Mia's heart twisted. "They're stuck inside a snow globe and Holly, the Patels' dog, is with them!" she explained. "It must be why I kept seeing Holly in snow. Aunt Carol told me she was going to test the globe. I think she tried out the magic on Holly—maybe because Mrs. Patel was one of Grandma Anne's friends and she wanted to hurt her, just like she's been trying to hurt me and my family. Now Bracken and Willow are trapped inside it, too."

Juniper chattered unhappily, and Sorrel bristled. "This is very bad news," she said. "If the elderly woman has them in her power, you'll have to do as she says."

"We've got to be able to stop her somehow," said Violet desperately.

At that moment, the cellar door opened.

"Hide!" Mia mouthed quickly.

Lexi hid behind the table while Violet ran to the wall and cast a glamour. She immediately seemed to merge with the wall. Juniper and Sorrel disappeared.

"Your friends will be here very soon," said Aunt Carol, coming down the stairs with the snow globe. She looked her usual self again. "But I don't think we need to wait for them to begin. It's time to start taking away your memories of magic." She touched the Dark Stone to the floor, and the circle around Mia and Sita vanished. "Who is going to be first?" she said with an evil smile.

A Shade stepped out from the shadows by the wall. It was tall and thin, with spiny fingers and sharp teeth. "How about me?" it hissed, flexing its fingers.

14
SHOWDOWN

Aunt Carol exclaimed in shock. Mia froze, but then she noticed the Shade had a glowing golden outline and realized it was Violet using her magic to cast an illusion.

"What are you doing here? Who conjured you from the shadows?" Aunt Carol backed away and stumbled on the Seeing Stone that Mia had thrown into the cellar earlier. Losing her balance, she fell to the ground.

There was a sudden blur of movement—it was Lexi darting out from behind the table.

She grabbed the snow globe from Aunt Carol's hands before the elderly lady realized what was happening.

"No!" shrieked Aunt Carol, scrambling after her on her hands and knees. But Lexi was already safely on the other side of the room, cradling the snow globe in her hands.

The Shade became Violet once more. "Smash the globe, Lexi!"

"If you do, the animals will disappear forever!" hissed Aunt Carol.

Violet hesitated, but then she shook her head. "No, I don't believe you. When we smashed the mirror, it *released* the Mirror Shade."

"Yes, and when the garden gnome smashed, it set the Wish Shade inside it free," said Lexi.

"You're right!" urged Juniper, leaping onto the table with the crystals. "Do it, Lexi!"

Aunt Carol held up the Dark Stone and opened her mouth.

Mia's heart leaped into her throat. She was sure Aunt Carol was going to use some sort of horrible power on Lexi. She couldn't let that happen. Throwing herself at Aunt Carol, she grabbed the stone and wrestled it out of her fingers. "Got it!" she gasped in triumph.

Aunt Carol's eyes glittered. "And so you have!" she spat. She pointed at Mia from the floor and screamed out a string of harsh-sounding words that Mia couldn't understand.

Mia felt the world spin, and then it seemed as though her head was getting lighter and lighter. Her thoughts grew fuzzy and confused, and all she could hear were the strange-sounding words. She sank down to her knees, still holding the Dark Stone in her hands.

"What's happening?" Mia heard Violet cry. "What's she doing to Mia?"

"Stop it!" Sita shouted, pointing at Aunt Carol. Her voice was suddenly strong and clear. "I command you to be silent!"

Aunt Carol's mouth opened and closed, but no sound came out. With a yowl, Sorrel pounced on the elderly lady's chest, and Lexi threw the globe onto the floor. There was a huge smash, and it exploded into a million pieces.

The next instant, Bracken and Willow were in the room with the girls. Bracken raced over

to Mia and started licking her face. Willow
charged to Sita's side and rubbed her head
against her. Holly, the spaniel, scurried under
the table fearfully.

Mia started to pet the fox, but then she
stopped. Why was she petting a fox? He seemed
very tame.

She looked around. Why was she in a cellar
with her friends? And why were there so many
animals? And why was that wildcat sitting on
poor Aunt Carol's chest and hissing furiously
at her? "What's happening?" she said in
confusion.

"Mia!" the fox said, nuzzling her cheek. "Are you all right?"

Mia blinked. She could have sworn she'd just heard him say her name. But that couldn't be right. Animals couldn't talk. She stood up and backed away from the fox. "What ... what's going on?" she said faintly. She realized she was holding a dark sparkling stone in her hand and dropped it.

The red squirrel raced over and grabbed it in his paws.

"Stay where you are, Aunt Carol. I command you to freeze!" Sita said to Aunt Carol as she lunged at the squirrel.

Aunt Carol stopped with a jerk.

"What's happening?" Violet said. "Why is Mia being weird?"

"I didn't silence Aunt Carol in time," said Sita. "I think she said the spell—and now Mia has forgotten everything about magic."

"Magic?" Mia echoed in confusion. "What

are you talking about? Magic isn't real."

Seeing her friends exchange horrified looks, she buried her face in her hands. This was all too weird. Her head felt like it was spinning, and she was filled with an intense sense of loss, but she didn't know what for.

All four animals bounded over to her.

"Mia, it's a spell!"

Looking up, she saw that it was the fox speaking. He was staring at her intently with unusual indigo eyes.

"You can still get your memories back," said the wildcat. "Fight against the spell."

"You can do it, Mia," said the deer.

"We need you," said the squirrel, jumping onto her shoulder and smoothing her hair with his little paws. "Please try."

All of the animals were talking now! How strange this was.

"What memories?" said Mia. "I don't understand."

The fox put his paws up on her legs. She petted him. It was strange—she felt as if she knew him really well.

"Mia—magic is real," said Lexi. "We're Star Friends."

"We've had a lot of adventures together," added Violet. "We've fought Shades and sent them back to the shadows. Please believe us."

Mia looked into her green eyes. Violet did usually tell the truth, and fuzzy memories were starting to flash into her head of she and her friends doing magic. She frowned.

"Mia," Sita said. "The other day, I promised I'd never use magic on you, but I'm going to break my promise. You made me believe in my magic powers earlier today, and now I'm going to make you do something—I'm going to make you listen. Mia, you must believe us.

Magic *is* real."

More images formed in Mia's head. She and
her friends in the clearing in the woods with
the four animals.... She and Violet chasing
after a gnome....Trying to catch little yellow
stretchy men with fangs....

"Magic *is* real?" she said slowly.

Bracken licked her. "Yes. Please believe."

She looked into his sparkling eyes, framed by
his soft, rusty red fur, and felt the memories get
stronger and more vivid. Crouching down, she
hugged him, and breathing in his sweet smell,
her confusion cleared like a fog lifting. "Of
course magic is real!" she said. "I'm your Star
Friend—you're my Star Animal!"

"Always," said Bracken, nuzzling into her.

"All the things I'm remembering—they
really happened, didn't they?" Mia said, looking
at the others.

"Yes!" Lexi, Violet, and Sita said together.

"It depends on what you're imagining, but I

presume so," said Sorrel dryly.

Mia felt a rush of love for all her friends and their animals. "Thank you for helping me," she said.

Bracken swung around and looked at Aunt Carol, who was still frozen, unable to move, her eyes flashing furiously. "And that's why Star Friends are better than people who use dark magic," he said triumphantly to her. "Star Friends and their animals trust and help each other—and when they do, they can defeat anything!"

Aunt Carol glared at him, still under the power of Sita's command to be silent.

"Where's the Dark Stone?" Mia said.

"I've got it," said Juniper.

Mia walked back to Aunt Carol. "Can you unfreeze her, Sita?"

"Are you sure?" Sita said.

"We've got to do something. We can't leave her frozen forever." Mia looked at Aunt Carol.

"We'll give you a chance. If we unfreeze you, you have to do what we say and promise never to use dark magic again." She glanced at Sita. "Unfreeze her."

Sita pointed at Aunt Carol. "You may move and speak."

"How dare you subdue me like that!" Aunt Carol hissed at Sita.

"Do you promise that you will never use dark magic again?" Mia said.

"No!" said Aunt Carol. Moving surprisingly quickly, she lunged for Juniper. He leaped away from her, keeping the stone safe.

"I command you to freeze!" cried Sita, pointing at her.

Aunt Carol froze once more.

"Face me," said Sita calmly. "And open your hands."

Aunt Carol did as she was told.

"Juniper, put the stone in Aunt Carol's hands," Sita said.

"What?" Mia, Lexi, and Violet exclaimed.

"Sita, what are you doing?" Willow said.

"It's the only thing we *can* do if we want to keep Westport safe," said Sita softly. "Aunt Carol, you will keep hold of the Dark Stone and say the spell to forget everything having to do with magic."

Aunt Carol tried to shake her head but couldn't. Only her eyes moved from side to side.

"Sita? Are you sure?" Lexi asked.

"It's using dark magic," said Juniper anxiously.

"It's making her use dark magic against herself," said Sita. She looked at them all steadily. "I really *am* sure this is the only way." Her voice rang with a new confidence. "We have to protect Westport."

"I agree with Sita," said Sorrel. The other animals nodded, too.

"Yes. Do it," Mia said.

"You may speak," said Sita to Aunt Carol.

"Others will come," Aunt Carol burst out in a rush. "You can stop me, but the town will not be safe. The clearing in the woods is a powerful magical place. You will face other threats more dangerous than me. You will—"

"Enough!" Sita commanded. "Say the spell that will make you forget! Say it now!"

Aunt Carol's mouth moved, and she looked like she was trying to keep it shut, but the harsh words burst out of her in a tangled stream.

The stone glowed for a moment, and then Aunt Carol's eyes clouded, and she looked around in confusion.

"It worked!" breathed Lexi.

"That was incredible, Sita," said Mia in awe.

"What's happening?" Aunt Carol said, looking dazed. "Why are we in my cellar?" She held out the Dark Stone. "And what's this?"

"That's mine," said Mia hurriedly, taking it from her. The stone felt icy cold and seemed to prickle her fingers. She shoved it in her pocket. She saw Holly still hiding under the table and had an idea. "We were here to help you with the decorations, and then we heard a noise down here—it was the Patels' missing dog. I don't know how she got in here, but we all came to get her and … then you banged your head."

Aunt Carol blinked. "What about all these other animals?"

The Star Animals vanished.

Aunt Carol blinked.

"What do you mean, Aunt Carol?" Mia asked innocently.

Aunt Carol rubbed her eyes. "I thought I saw wild animals…. My goodness, I really did bang my head, didn't I?"

"You did. How about we go upstairs, and we can make you a cup of tea?" Lexi said.

"I think that would be a good idea," said Aunt Carol faintly.

"And then we should take Holly home to the Patels," said Sita, crouching down and holding her hand out to the spaniel. "Come here, Holly. It's okay now. Come out."

Holly crept out, and Sita picked her up. The spaniel licked her face, immediately calming down as Sita petted and soothed her.

"The Christmas fair!" said Aunt Carol suddenly. "I need to take the decorations there."

"Don't worry. We'll take care of that for you," said Mia as they went upstairs. "You can rest and come to the fair later, when you're feeling better."

Aunt Carol smiled. "That's very kind of you, dears. Thank you very much."

15
TIME TO PLAY!

"What are we going to do about the
decorations?" Mia whispered to the others
when Aunt Carol was settled with a cup of tea.
"We can't let them be sold at the fair."

"I have an idea," said Lexi. She turned
to Aunt Carol and picked up one of the
decorations. "Um, I think there might be a
problem with these decorations."

"What kind of problem?" Aunt Carol said.

"It's the crystals in the center of the eyes. I
showed the decoration you gave me to my mom,

and she said it's a choking hazard for children."

Aunt Carol looked worried. "Oh, dear, I hadn't thought of that. I put them on because … because…." She frowned. "Well, I think I thought they looked pretty. Yes, that must be why."

"We could always take them off for you," said Lexi. "The decorations will look just as cute without the sparkly crystals."

"It really would be best," Violet added quickly as Aunt Carol hesitated.

"If you don't mind," said Aunt Carol. "It's a shame—but I would hate for a child to get hurt."

The four girls worked quickly. Soon, all of the crystals were sealed in a bag that Bracken buried deep in a flower bed in the yard, and the decorations were nothing more than just normal Christmas decorations.

"We'll take them to the town hall," said Sita. "And we'll take Holly home on the way."

They created a makeshift leash for Holly using a piece of thick ribbon from Aunt Carol's sewing box and then waved good-bye to Aunt Carol.

When they reached the Patels', the family was overjoyed to see Holly.

"Where did you find her?" Mrs. Patel asked as her two little girls hugged the spaniel in delight, and Holly bounded around them.

"In the woods," Mia said. They'd all decided that that would be the best story.

"Thank you so much for bringing her back," said Mrs. Patel.

"No problem!" the girls chorused.

The girls went to the town hall and delivered the decorations. Mia's mom was already there. "I'm very glad you're here, girls," she said. "We could use some extra help."

They were immediately swept up into getting the hall ready, the booths set up, and the coffee things arranged in the kitchen. At two o'clock, the hall doors were opened, and people flocked in. Soon, the whole place was full of people buying gifts, drinking tea and coffee, eating cakes, and chatting. The smell of gingerbread and cotton candy filled the air.

Mia's mom came up to her with Alex. He was wearing a Santa Claus hat and eating iced gingerbread. "The fair is going so well," said her mom happily. "Grandma Anne would be really happy to know that everything was continuing just as she would have wanted."

"Mmm-hmm," Mia said, glancing over at where Aunt Carol was selling her decorations. She had a feeling her grandma would be even more happy to know that they had managed to stop Aunt Carol's evil plans!

We'll have to keep a close eye on her in case the spell wears off, Mia thought. *And we need to think about what to do with the Dark Stone.*

"Do you want to buy some gingerbread to have with your friends?" her mom said. "Violet, Lexi, and Sita are over there." She got some money out of her purse.

"Thanks, Mom! Is it okay if we go for a walk?" Mia said.

"Sure. I'll see you back at home later."

Mia ran to join the others, and they bought slabs of warm gingerbread covered with sweet white icing and then headed for the clearing, munching happily. No one said a thing about what had happened with Aunt Carol. It was as though they all had a silent agreement not to speak about it until they reached the privacy of the clearing and could call their Star Animals.

They hurried down the track, past Grandma Anne's house with a "For Sale" sign up and along the overgrown footpath. Dark green ivy

scrambled through the holly bushes, with their red berries providing splashes of color against all the dull green and brown.

As they hurried into the clearing, the girls called their animals' names, and the four Star Animals appeared. Willow bucked joyfully, Juniper raced up a tree, Sorrel rolled onto her back in a patch of winter sunlight, and Bracken chased his bushy tail.

"We did it!" said Sita, breathing a sigh of relief.

"Yep," said Violet. "Although we must remember to get rid of the decorations in our houses, too."

"And from my grandma's," said Sita.

Mia nodded. "Once we've gotten rid of them—and decided what to do with the Dark Stone—everyone will be safe."

"Until some new threat comes along," said Lexi. "Do you think Aunt Carol was right, and more evil will come here?"

"If it does, we'll stop it!" Violet declared.

"I'm sure you'll be able to, Violet," Sorrel said, weaving between her legs. "You saved the day today by turning into that Shade. And it was you who realized you could smash the globe."

Mia waited for Lexi to roll her eyes as she usually did when Sorrel boasted about Violet, but she didn't. She smiled and linked arms with Violet. "Sorrel's right—you were amazing, Violet."

"It wasn't just me," said Violet. "You were amazing when you snatched the Dark Stone, and Mia was amazing when she fought off the magic spell…."

"Only thanks to all of you," Mia put in.

"You were awesome, too, Sita," Violet went on. "If you hadn't commanded Aunt Carol, I don't know what would have happened."

Sita blushed. "I wouldn't have been able to do it without Mia. She made me realize why the magic wasn't working. I just had to believe."

Mia glanced around and remembered something Aunt Carol had said. "Is this clearing really powerful like Aunt Carol told us, Bracken? Will it attract other people wanting to do dark magic?"

"It might," said Bracken. "It's a crossing place—a place where the Star World and the human world meet. It contains a lot of power…."

"And power will always attract people who

want to use it for their own evil ends," said Sorrel seriously. "We must all be on our guard."

"But those people aren't here yet," said Juniper. "So for now, let's play!" He scampered away and Lexi raced after him, using her magic to climb a tree just as fast as him.

"Who wants to play a game of tag?" she called, hanging down from a branch.

"Me!" said Violet to Mia's surprise. "Only if I can shadow-travel though," she added with a grin. "You're way too fast otherwise."

"Okay," said Lexi. "Catch me if you can!" She swung through the branches before dropping down to the clearing floor. She landed in a patch of shadows and squealed as Violet popped right up and tagged her.

"Got you!" Violet said, laughing.

Sita giggled. "One–nil Violet," she said, sitting down on a tree stump and putting her arm over Willow's back. "Willow and I will keep score! We don't have a chance of keeping up with you." Willow snuggled against her happily.

Bracken nestled into Mia's arms and licked her face.

"I'm so glad I didn't lose you today," she told him, remembering how awful she had felt when she thought she might never see him again.

He wriggled deeper into her arms. "I hated being stuck in that snow globe and not being able to get to you. I never want that to happen again."

Mia hugged him tightly. "It won't. We'll keep each other safe."

"Forever," Bracken promised. "Whatever comes."

Mia's heart swelled joyfully. She loved being able to do magic with Lexi,

Violet, and Sita, and being able to help and protect people, but most of all, she loved having Bracken as her Star Animal.

"I love you," she whispered to him.

He squirmed in delight and licked her nose.

"Come on, Mia!" shouted Lexi. "Come and play!"

Mia grinned at Bracken. "Should we join in?"

He nodded and jumped down from her arms. Bounding across the clearing, he leaped on top of Sorrel. "Time to play, pussycat!"

Sorrel yowled indignantly and sprang to her feet. Bracken tried to run away, but Sorrel was too fast. They rolled across the ground play-fighting while Willow shook her head and Juniper scampered around them excitedly.

Bursting with happiness, Mia ran to join her friends.

About the Author

Linda Chapman is the best-selling author of more than 200 books. The biggest compliment she can have is for a child to tell her he or she became a reader after reading one of her books. She lives in a cottage with a tower in Leicestershire, England, with her husband, three children, three dogs, and three ponies. When she's not writing, Linda likes to ride, read, and visit schools and libraries to talk to people about writing.

About the Illustrator

Lucy Fleming has been an avid doodler and bookworm since early childhood. Drawing always seemed like so much fun, but she never dreamed it could be a full-time job! She lives and works in a small town in England with her partner and a little black cat. When not at her desk, she likes nothing more than to be outdoors in the sunshine with a cup of hot tea.